Whatever Happens, Probably Will

Stories

John W. MacIlroy

ISBN: 978-1-7923-7230-8 (paperback)
ISBN: 978-1-7923-7231-5 (hardcover)
ISBN: 978-1-7923-7244-5 (e-book)
Library of Congress Control Number: 2021914903

Printed in the United States of America

First edition publisher: Short Story America
Visit us online at www.shortstoryamerica.com

Cover Photography: Amir Bajric
Design: Soundview Design

To my grandchildren
Tucker Whittington,
Emma Grace,
and Elizabeth Lee

Whatever Happens, Probably Will

Stories

"**Whatever Happens, Probably Will** is a splendidly varied collection of stories. All of these tales deserve to be read at least twice. Bravo to John W. MacIlroy!"

—*John Engell, Professor Emeritus of American Literature, Film, and Creative Writing,* **San Jose State University**

—⚭—

"**Whatever Happens, Probably Will** offers the very best in a short story collection. This is all-in-one-sitting entertainment, with eighteen full-bodied tales that birth characters and places you will not soon forget. You will journey to a failing tavern in a tiny New England town where a curious barkeep named Bump O'Rourke discovers that 'cash flow is not magic,' although other things just may be; to a midwestern suburb to meet Dan and Sharon Pritchard for dinner in their white colonial along a quiet street lined with tall oaks, middling ambitions and short mailboxes; to the Mississippi Delta where Boone Chandler, a much-married man, is about to tie the knot with Number Six, or is it Seven? With a folksy tone and a deft insertion of the ominous within the common—spotting an injured barn swallow in the foothills of the Blue Ridge, picking bright blue hydrangeas in a back garden of a Charleston home—these stories pull at the heart, with essences and end notes as satisfying as a fine wine. A prose *maestro*, MacIlroy finds the poignancy, and often the absurdity, in our journeys. Be prepared to feel everything."

—*Elizabeth Robin, winner of the 2021 Carrie McCray Nickens Fellowship and author of* **To My Dreamcatcher**, **Where Green Meets Blue**, *and* **Silk Purses and Lemonade**

—⚭—

"*Whatever Happens, Probably Will*, the startling debut collection from John W. MacIlroy, is sprinkled with tales of wonder and a touch of wistfulness. These stories call us to find hope in the everyday, meaning in the bittersweet, and strength in a punch to the gut. Along the way, especially in lighter tales like "The Closer," MacIlroy delivers belly laughs deserving of the best.

—*Andrew Clark, author of* **Jesus in the Trailer**

—⚬—

"Writing with sensitivity and humor, John W. MacIlroy's stories delight in the mischievous turn of phrase, powering on to endings that bring both heartbreak and joy, often wrapped in a wicked twist. In some of the stories, like my favorite "The Painting," we feel the long and heavy shadow of the past, and the pain that haunts at the edge of the ordinary life. In others, like "Slim Chance" and "Customer Service," we take a lighter journey, the author reminding us of the quiet nonsense of the everyday. And in the end, his writing simply leaves you wanting more."

—*Midge Pierce, media consultant, former publicist at* **Simon & Schuster**

—⚬—

"Get ready to smile. Not just because of the humor in many of John W. MacIlroy's stories, though there's plenty of that. But because he's writing about you. Yes, you. Whoever you are, you'll find yourself in every one of these stories. You're the kid playing ball, the young man going off to war, the person trying to get someone at the bank to answer your call. And it's not just because you recognize the events, it's because you recognize the feelings. The frustrations, the bemusements, the sadness, the happiness, the longings, the joy. If you want to read about yourself, read a John W. MacIlroy story."

—*Barry Dickson, author of* **Maybe Today**

—⁐—

"John W. MacIlroy's ability to evoke a certain landscape, period, emotion, or character is dead-on. He creeps up like fog on a page, weaving a spell around his readers and drawing them into his world of fiction, suspended disbelief and all. He illuminates the fortunate, the forgotten, the sinners, the has-beens and the broken with equally deft strokes. And he injects his reader—vividly and physically—into each setting. You'll feel the fingers of Spanish Moss graze the back of your neck on a Mississippi bluff, stare into the dark along the rural Georgia train track, smell the stale beer in a forgotten mill-town bar, shudder with a sudden chill as you look out the cabin window of the redeye to Boston, hear the echoes of a once-great baseball team, taste the sweet wine of a long-shared life as the sun slips toward the horizon. The best way to read MacIlroy is to relax, surrender, and fasten your seatbelt. You are about to be transported by a master storyteller. Enjoy the ride!"

—Jayne Adams, author of the forthcoming short story collection **For All the Right Seasons**

—⁐—

"Let yourself fall into these pages 'where a tall tale is as likely to be served up as shrimp and grits to those traveling through.' You'll believe these tales, tall or not—and you'll savor them all. You'll be haunted by the image of three 'olive drab' buses waiting to carry young men to meet their fate. You'll be drawn into a baseball game's mysterious timelessness that may have slipped outside the boundaries of the field. And your heart will break at a boy's love for the father he had never seen—a love that, for him, was 'like trying to capture a firefly on a hot summer night.' You'll smile at the misadventures of a clergyman with 'dusty charm and a charitable understanding of the tides of marriage.' And you'll laugh in commiseration with the woes of poor Richard 'Ferbie' Frobush as he tries to circumnavigate a customer service call. John W.

MacIlroy is a master of the moment—the moment when everything turns, and the reader suddenly and deeply knows the heart of the character who is, all at once, not so different from the reader herself."

—*Beverly Jean Harris, runner-up for the **Short Story America Prize for Short Fiction***

—∿—

"With his new collection of short stories, **Whatever Happens, Probably Will**, John W. MacIlroy has written a quintessentially American book. From the Revolutionary War to the Covid-19 pandemic, MacIlroy's tales will take you on an engaging tour of American life and history that is by turns touching, hair-raising, and hilarious. These are profoundly compassionate stories of struggle and resilience, of average people confronting the odds that are always stacked against average people. You'll meet ghostly ballplayers, faithful custodians, starry-eyed youngsters, grieving parents, heartbroken lovers, and many more, in a cast of characters you won't soon forget. You'll recognize their very American dreams and the American landscapes in which their lives unfold. MacIlroy weaves these riches together and spins his tales with the skill of a born storyteller who also happens to be gifted with a poet's eye. By all means, dig in to this wonderful collection. Every page will surprise and delight you."

—*Douglas Campbell, winner of the **Able Muse Write Prize for Fiction***

Contents

"Crawling at your feet," said the Gnat, "you may observe a
    Bread-and-Butterfly. Its wings are thin slices of bread-
    and butter, its body is a crust."
"And what does it live on?"
"Weak tea with cream in it."
    A new difficulty came into Alice's head. "Supposing it
    couldn't find any?"
"Then it would die of course."
"But that must happen very often," Alice said thoughtfully.
"It always happens," said the Gnat.

—Lewis Carroll, **Through the Looking Glass**

The Painting

—ᵐᵐ—

Maddie Cheever tilted her head back, then sideways. "Too low, and crooked."

"You sure? People hang paintings too high." But Taylor Longworth Cheever—*Tad* to everyone but his wife of almost nineteen years—knew when to let things slide. He removed the painting, pounded in a new nail, then rehung it a few inches higher, centering it precisely above a tall vase on the foyer table.

"Better?"

Maddie nodded, and brushed some dust off the oversized gilded frame. The painting, a somewhat boxy oil composition, featured an old car—those who know such things would guess it, correctly, a 1946 Ford Woody, with its distinctive light birds-eye maple trim and darker mahogany side panels—sitting in front of a white shingle-shake carriage house. On the Woody's driver's-side door, in a gracefully-scripted half arc, was *Cheever Timber*. A young girl, maybe twelve or thirteen, leaned out an open dormer window of the house. She was smiling, her long blond hair just brushing the sill.

The whole thing had a curious primitive charm, like a Grandma Moses townscape, although the angles of the house were all wrong, and the Woody itself squat and too small. The impression was one of artistic promise as yet unfulfilled.

And in the lower right corner, in careful slanting letters, the artist had signed the work: *Maddie Weeks Cheever*.

"She'll like it there." Maddie paused. "I'll bring in some fresh hydrangeas from the garden, for the vase—just her favorite blue ones, don't you think?" Tad tried to smile. He had not wanted to hang the picture at all.

Maddie went on before he said anything. "Yes." She paused. "Yes, she'll like them, too. I know she will."

—∞—

Tad Cheever had always been rich—boarding-school rich—swimming in old southern timber-money and trust funds, and spending his summers at his family's private hunting lodge near Squirrel Creek, Georgia.

Maddie Weeks had never been rich, at least not until her marriage. Her father still managed the lodge, with her mother cooking for the Cheever clan. Ask around, and folks will tell you Jennie Weeks' tangy Brunswick stew is still the best along the coast. Maddie was raised on the second floor of the property's carriage house, her dormer bedroom directly above the stall where the Ford was garaged. Maddie was two months younger than Tad, strong-willed and country-smart, her hair the deep-red of a rust-streaked tin roof, her eyes large and jade green, flecked with gold. She grew up sassy and fast among the soft whispers of the tall Georgia pine.

In the summers when he was back from school, she would lean out her bedroom window and watch Taylor—she never called him Tad, even when they were children—wax the Ford in a shady area next to the house.

It wasn't long before he started to notice Maddie Weeks, too.

A week after her eighteenth birthday, on an old blanket spread hurriedly in the back of the car and smelling like stale wool, they made fumbling, desperate, *forever* love.

And it was there, on a rainy afternoon seven weeks later, that she told him she was pregnant. On a small desk in her dormer bedroom, directly above where they sat in the Woody, was an acceptance letter from the Savannah College of Art and Design.

—⟋⟍—

Maddie stared at the painting. "I don't think I got Caroline's hair quite right, do you?"

"You did fine, Maddie."

"But she'll understand, won't she?"

Tad reached out to her, but she was already walking away.

—⟋⟍—

"How's she doing, Tad?" The voice on his phone was tired, the conversation practiced and sad.

"About the same," He paused. "No, Mother. The truth is, today's a bad day." He hesitated. "She wanted it up again."

"But didn't they tell you the painting would only—"

"Yes, they did." He hesitated, unsure of what to say next. "You know we all loved the carriage house, Caroline most of all. She would poke all around the place, listening to her grampa's stories, tasting her nana's cornbread, always asking about the Ford." Tad's voice broke. "One day she looked at me, kind of funny, and said: '*In the Woody? Really?*' She was all giggles, Mother, but I knew she was growing up so fast."

He looked at the three silver-framed photos of his daughter, placed neatly on the corner of his desk.

In one she is standing under a licorice-twisted branch of an old live oak, pretending to hold it up with one arm. She looked to be about eleven, taken when they all went to the Old Sheldon Church ruins near Yemassee. In the second, she and Maddie are standing on a low wooden dock jutting into a tidal creek, both pointing to a marsh hen hitching a ride on a mat of floating spartina grass, and Tad remembered how Maddie had worried that their daughter, then just seven, would jump in after it. And in the third—the only one in color—Caroline is standing with five other girls, all in sun dresses of pink and blue and yellow. It was taken three years earlier at a birthday party in the back garden of their Charleston home, on Legare.

It was her sixteenth, and her last.

"You know, Mother, Caroline loved posing for the painting. She told me once that when Maddie was mixing her paints she would close her eyes and think of her mom in that very window on a hot Georgia summer day years ago *'just reelin' in'*—that's what she said—*'just reelin' in that rich Cheever boy—'* "

Taylor Longworth Cheever—still a rich man, folks say—put down the phone.

Out the window of his study he saw his wife in the garden, cutting only hydrangeas of the brightest blue.

Duke's

"Here's the thing, deVereux."

I didn't hear Punch Stallings come up behind me. I never do. He is an overripe hulk of a man, a former all-conference tackle at Clemson now tending toward the soft and mushy from the good life at the Awkward Oyster, the marsh-side place we own just north of Brunswick, along the Georgia intra-coastal.

It's nothing fancy: sandwiches, a funky selection of beers, a good crowd of regulars—mostly the local shrimpers and mill shift-workers at International Paper. Twice each fall we put on an oyster roast that also pulls in the fancier BMW crowd staying over at the Cloisters on Sea Island, and Punch runs around introducing himself as the *Executive Chef.*

I just let it go.

We nearly lost it all a couple years ago, whacked by a late-season storm that slammed nearly headlong into the place, and then we were nearly smothered by a nasty balloon-mortgage. But the old pilings held, First Carolina Coastal re-financed, and we re-opened with a new tin roof, some fresh paint, a hint of cash in our pockets, and a Friday night all-you-can-eat ribs special for $12.99. The ribs were a hit, and when Punch threw in blended rye shots for a buck a couple weeks later—top shelf only—the locals dubbed it "ribs, rye and regrets." Punch jumped on it, plastering the whole thing up in big capital letters on our specials' board behind the bar, crowning it as a regular Friday night blow-out. Business has never been better.

Punch certainly has a head for all this, and we get along well enough. But he can be… annoying. First, he always calls me by my last name, even though I'm married to his cousin, and it drives her crazy too. Second, he just *appears*. His movements defy logic, along with the laws of gravity and the physics of mass, his impressive bulk floating through the air like the Goodyear blimp until he drifts in for a mooring, silently, right behind you. And third, he starts just about every conversation with…

"Here's the thing."

He was at it again. "I found a half-eaten pastrami sandwich, back of the kitchen. Fourth time this week."

"Some people eat light, Punch." He let that go, but wasn't finished. He never is.

"It wasn't made with mustard, but *with mayonnaise*, don't you see? Duke's, I'm sure. On white bread, no pickles." He started shaking. "*With lettuce and tomato*. Nobody makes a pastrami sandwich like that." He paused. "Nobody but that new guy, McCollister."

—⁂—

Jefferson McCollister had come up from somewhere near Macon, not long out of the army and on the drift. He had served a tour in Iraq and was looking for a job. We needed another short order cook, something he had done in the army although he didn't elaborate. He was hard-working, kept to himself, and put up with Punch.

I liked him. Punch didn't.

"The freaking sandwich looks like a BLT." Punch wasn't finished. "Two days ago I saw McCollister make, *then actually eat*, a mayonnaise sandwich, nothing but the mayo and bread."

I held back because I'm pretty much addicted to mayonnaise, too. Duke's, of course, Hellmann's in a pinch. But Punch, on some frolic and detour a few years back, had worked at a deli in Brooklyn. He returned with some strange Yankee ways, including a curious obsession with Gulden's Spicy Brown Mustard and the movie reviews of the *New*

Yorker, although few of their picks ever make it to the screen at the Highway 21 Dixie Drive-In up the road.

"All right, I'll talk to him." I'm always amazed the crap that comes with running this place.

—⁂—

"What's goin' on, Mr. deVereux?"

"Little dust-up with Punch this afternoon." I shrugged. "You do know most folks around here like a pastrami sandwich made with mustard, right?" I smiled, just to let him know I was the good guy here. "Look, I'm kind of a mayonnaise guy too. But mostly on a BLT."

"Duke's?"

I nodded.

Jefferson paused. "Can I tell you a story?"

"Sure."

"In Iraq I bunked next to a tough corporal named Mullins, just turned twenty. He was a country boy from Georgia too, and his mom sent him a couple jars of Duke's every month, and we would heap gobs of the stuff on everything. Hamburgers, hot dogs, French fries. Even mixed it into spaghetti, but just once." He smiled. "But it wasn't really about the mayonnaise; it was all about *home*. It could have been mustard, or sweet tea, or almost about anything else. It just happened to be mayonnaise."

He paused. "But Mullins, well, he loved it on a pastrami sandwich, on white bread." Jefferson slowed a beat. "He was about halfway through one when the Lieutenant pulled him for a quick recon mission, kind of routine, no big deal. He asked me to wrap it up, hold it for him." Jefferson looked away. "You see, Mr. deVereux, he never made it back."

I didn't know what to say, so I said nothing.

"Now, every day I can, I make a pastrami sandwich. I go heavy on the mayo, and load it up with other stuff we didn't always have over there. I only eat half, and leave the other half for my friend, just in case..." Jefferson's voice broke. "Look, I know that's kind of..."

He turned away, then back to me.

"It's just something I have to do."

Three Buses, Waiting

Stephen Westcutt remembers the gray of the day, how they all pen-guin-walked single file, awkwardly trying to straddle the industrial safety-tape which snaked around the cold wooden second floor of the nothing building like a bad imitation of the yellow brick road. He re-members how the whole place smelled like the nurse's office in his old grade school, how they were naked much of the time, and how that day they all said goodbye to childhood.

Stephen's wife would remind him that he used to talk about the fat white kid behind him in that line, the kid who wore the bright or-ange boxers sporting little yellow m&m's dancing in a pattern across wrinkled cotton. A single yellow m&m on the front was dressed like an oversized Mr. Potato Head, complete with crossed-eyes, tiny arms, and a wide black "Have a Nice Day" smile long before it appeared every-where, the whole thing a spectacularly poor choice for the morning, everything considered.

Stephen has, however, learned to distrust his memory, as old men must. So maybe he's wrong about how long they were completely na-ked, and a few other things about that day as well.

But he is quite sure about the sign in the foyer of the building that morning. It sat on a wooden easel, a cheap black-felt-and-grooved poster-sized display set with those annoyingly easy-to-lose white small-case plastic letters.

The sign informed those who needed it that that they had found their way to the *Military Examination and Induction CenteR, Floor 2,* the army apparently as quick to lose those tiny lower-case letters as everybody else.

The building itself was a humorless relic on a busy street. It had once been a successful leather tannery, then something to do with the old Wiss Scissors Company, and finally a struggling piece-goods shop before the city bought it in the mid-fifties. All this he had learned just that morning from a well-worn brass plaque next to the entrance door as he paused a moment before going in.

A letter tucked in the back pocket of his chino pants promised that his prompt arrival on the second floor of that humorless building, at 9:30 on the morning of November 20, 1967, would reward him with a comprehensive personal medical exam, courtesy of a grateful nation. He is sure that it was signed in a fussy backward-slanting script by a Mr. T. D. Hubert, Acting Head of his local draft board, as the letter now lives in an old cigar box on the top shelf of his bedroom closet.

And Stephen Westcutt is also sure that the kid in front of him that morning in November was skinnier than he had ever imagined anyone could be.

Or at least as skinny as anyone who could soon be humping his weight in combat gear through a steamy jungle somewhere halfway around the world, in a war no one understood, a war with a rabid hunger for boys who were not yet men.

—⁘—

The impossibly skinny kid was tall, black, thin-shouldered, eighteen or nineteen tops. He looked much younger, Stephen had thought, like an underweight high school freshman hoping to make the cross-country team.

Stephen was none of that: short, broad-shouldered, twenty-one by a week, and white. He had always looked old for his age—a useful asset for a suburban kid back when he and his underage buddies would drive a few miles to a smoky saloon with a most accommodating view of the drinking age. When the tired guy behind the bar asked to see some proof, Stephen would shrug, then pull out a smartly-doctored and premium-purchased fake license. The beers soon flowed freely, and always with a wink.

Everyone was in on the deal—or at least the kids from the leafier suburbs, the luckier ones with six-year-old Chevies, a couple bucks in their pockets, and promises of a sweet college deferment, even at some jerkwater junior outfit in the Ozarks.

But, like most deals, not everybody was in.

And in that penguin-walking line they all knew it.

—⁓—

The floor sagged toward the windows on the east side of the building, the side with the larger industrial windows. Along the wall, orderlies in pale blue scrubs and army-issue buzz cuts were busily asking questions and recording what they learned in triplicate on oversize clipboards. The penguin-walk stopped there for a minute, the flow of paperwork choking on its own bureaucratic logic, and Stephen looked out.

In the far distance he saw the Pabst Brewery, along the Parkway on the city's western border. The huge water tower atop the sprawling building, hugging the low gray cloud ceiling, was painted—Jersey-famous and justly so, Stephen has long thought—exactly like a dark brown bottle of Pabst Blue Ribbon, its bright label proudly telling the world that it was *The Original.*

Just down the block he could see a small liquor store and what might have been a grocer, mostly scorched timber and broken glass and piles of ash. Mortally wounded in the summer riots, both were partially wrapped in a layer of plywood, sloppy graffiti of the ugliest sort mocking the well-centered CONDEMNED painted on the wood in large letters the color of dried blood.

And directly under the windows he saw the three buses.

They were parked neatly at an angle to the building, and dressed in the olive drab of the Army of the United States. Sometimes he remembers their doors as open, but he is no longer sure. He has learned that it is only the young who can't distinguish between the open doors that invite and the open doors that menace.

What he does know—and knew then—was that most of the kids on the second floor of that nothing building in the fall of 1967 would not be going home that night, but heading down the road on those buses to Fort Dix, the Army's basic training center for the newly-conscripted.

Some of them would not be going home, ever.

—∞—

There would one day be a book—many books really—about that line of boys in nothing buildings all across the country that autumn, and how few things are really ever fair. But it would not be Stephen's book to write. *The Matterhorn*, written by a Marine who served in Vietnam, would be the one he would recommend to those who still did not understand the horribly skewed class and racial burdens of the war, and how it all began on the second floors of nothing buildings across the country, and then unraveled ugly thousands of miles away.

But that day in Newark—Stephen knows it now—he should have seen it coming.

Maybe everyone should have seen it coming.

Of those sixty boys penguin-walking the yellow taped line, he would have bet that fewer than a dozen had those prized college deferments in hand, and he would have collected on that bet. They were the slightly older ones, in their early twenties, commanded to the inner city by some jurisdictional quirk of Local Draft Board No. 16, its greedy reach sweeping west beyond the meaner streets of the city, and then a few miles into the leafier suburban neighborhoods just beyond. Many years later, Stephen would tell his wife that his drive home that day looked much like the opening credit sequence of *The Sopranos*, its message clear.

Things are never the same for everyone.

—∞—

Stephen Westcutt will tell you that the buses parked in parade rest under those windows were all part of the deal, and he wishes they had not been. The image haunts him still.

He knew, you see, that those buses were not for him.

He moved on past the windows, into a morning of poking and prodding and coughing in that special way until someone just before lunch informed him that he had passed his physical, but was free to go—his college deferment armed to do its magic for another eight months.

Who knows what happens then? That's what he wondered.

But his buddies had promised him a cold beer that night, and they made good. Stephen didn't talk much about his day: the drinks were cold and cheap, the place lively, the evening riding on the beer-frothy promise of another tomorrow. On the way to the restroom hard into the evening he noticed a bright neon Pabst Blue Ribbon sign on the back wall.

He had not noticed it before. It made him sad.

—∞—

Stephen Westcutt spends much time now, as old men do, arranging and re-arranging the pieces of his life—trimming and cutting here, buffing and smoothing there. He hopes he is asking the right questions and looking in the right places for the answers, although time for choices—the big ones anyway—is long gone. Perhaps, he thinks, that is the way it must be.

But he is no longer surprised by the stuff which clings to the margins.

He can tell you—not that anyone is ever likely to ask him—that on the day of his draft physical, November 20, 1967, the United States Census Bureau reported that the population of the country had reached 200 million, precisely at 11:03 in the morning, Eastern Standard Time. He would know this because he looked it up, but that was many years later and for no real reason.

He can tell you that just over three weeks later the Silver Bridge over the Ohio River at Point Pleasant, West Virginia, collapsed, killing 46 people. He would know this because one of those lost was a second cousin, on his mother's side.

He can tell you that soon thereafter Otis Redding died in a plane crash, because everyone knows that.

He can also tell you that by the end of that year, 228,263 boys had been drafted into the military service.

And he can tell you that he was not one of them.

He thinks about that often now, a man now living alone along a tidal creek in the Lowcountry of South Carolina. Two or three times a week he takes a walk along the high grass of the marsh to a quaint community park, a celebration of the natural world not far from his one-bedroom condo. He has done that for almost a year now. He likes to sit on the same bench and watch the world tumble on, quiet thoughts his usual companion.

A small veterans' memorial sits at the back of the park, with a brick walkway winding around in a half-circle. He watches folks stop to look for a name—or maybe several—engraved on those bricks. He watches others linger to read a polished brass plaque under the flagpole honoring those who never came home from the wars. He sees that they are often older, men mostly—at least the ones in the dark blue baseball caps with their branch of the service stitched on the crown, or the name of a ship, or the bright yellow, red and green of the Vietnam-service ribbon. He sees more of these now.

Wars end, they say.

He looks at the old men, and their hats, and their sad walk around the bricks, and he is not so sure about that. He is always quick to thank them, the ones with the hats as they walk by. Especially the ones in the yellow, red and green.

Stephen Westcutt then closes his eyes.

He sees three buses, a burned-out liquor store, an enormous bottle of Pabst Blue Ribbon hugging a gray sky. Absurd and grotesque, it looms over everything he remembers of that day, like the haunt of the knowing eyes of Dr. T.J. Eckleburg.

Rising above the ashes of the wounded city, the bottle sees all too.

And then—always *then*—Stephen Westcutt sees a fat white kid and a skinny black kid penguin-walking toward the menacing darkness that always summons the less fortunate. And he wonders what happened to them, the day he lost his innocence winding around the second floor of a nothing building in a broken city, in the sad fall of his twenty-first year.

The Closer

"Seven times. That your lucky number?"

He knew that voice, always a bit loud. He turned, and saw she was walking toward him from the porch where the other wedding guests had gathered.

"Six. It will be just *six*, Katherine."

Katherine had been Boone Chandler's second wife. The years since their brief marriage had yielded not only a truce, but an easy friendship which was the envy of their many friends whose marriages had also hit the rocks. Time had been kind to Katherine, and no one was surprised that she had come to watch her former husband set sail again—or that she had brought along a young buck.

"Kat..."

Katherine held up her hands. "Yeah, Boone, I know. You and that harpy Vicki just took a little time-out before she made her encore. But you divorced her, then re-married her. That counts as *two* marriages, even under the new math."

She was having fun, and Boone knew it.

"Let's run the numbers again." She began to tick them off. "There was Billie, your starter bride. Then me. Vicki in for round one, and then that mousy young Ashley from upstate, briefly. Vicki round two, back for just a year, followed by Sandra. Divorces all." Katherine paused to look around for her young buck, who seemed a bit too interested in the caterer's assistant at the far end of the porch where she was fussing with the wine glasses. "Elizabeth is batter-up for number *seven*, buddy."

Boone had been through the same math a month ago when the pastor at the local Reformed Pentecostal Church had declined to do the marriage, suggesting a *better fit* for the ceremony would be the Reverend H. James Lauderton.

"He'll get the job done for you," his pastor promised.

—m—

The Reverend Lauderton was the last to arrive, running late from an earlier ceremony in the next county. He parked his dusty pick-up near the ancient live oaks that had framed the old house for almost two centuries, just a few yards way. He knew that Beau—his nine-year old chocolate lab fast asleep on the torn seat next to him—would like the shade of those live oaks, their branches draping heavily over each end of the long front porch, wisps of Spanish moss just kissing the dark green tin roof.

As he struggled out of the old Ford, a loose thread popped an overworked shirt button just above his impressive waist. It spiraled to the ground, landing next to a small brass plaque set on a rough cut-stone marker honoring the very spot where the younger brother of the ancestral owner—the bride's great grandfather—had fallen long ago, a Yankee bullet in his belly. The trees had stood vigil for well over a century, bearing witness not only to the ravages of time and war and disease but to the many mischiefs and follies of man as well.

The Reverend had seen his share, too.

He picked up the button and stuffed it into his suit pocket. He had met Boone only once, and briefly, most arrangements having been made hastily by phone. But he was quick to pick out the groom: Boone was a devilishly handsome late fifties, a full head of silver-white hair curling in the back coupled with a smile deserving of the nickname hung on him by one of the few young ladies in town he had not ac-tually married—*Lord Smiley*. A small white carnation was pinned to his dark blue suit, and he was pacing. The bride, who looked about twenty-five years Boone's junior, was chatting with guests on the other end of the porch. She looked calm.

Good. That's half the battle, the Reverend thought. He walked over to the groom.

"Sorry I cut it a little close."

"Just glad to see you, Padre." They shook hands.

"You all set?"

"Yeah, sure." Boone paused. "I mean, I think so."

The Reverend had seen this all before. A last-minute panic, a need to tidy up the account before that next step. In fact, just that morning he had married a couple over in Copiah County who had gone *double digit* in the marital metrics, although he was sure one of them—the bride, this time—was going to bolt before he could get them over the finish line. It had required a little creative scripture, but he closed the deal.

That was the thing about the Reverend H. James Lauderton: he always seemed to come up with something. He turned to Boone and put his arm on his shoulder. "I think you need a little *comfort* from the Good Book." The Reverend worked up his best holy face and deepened his voice. "Do you remember the Parable of the Shepherd and the Feast?"

Boone nodded, although he had no clue what Lauderton was talking about.

The Reverend began. "*That man shall take on thy mate for the fullness of the Seven Moons, alas until the Gathering of the Great Feast and the darkening of the sky.*"

This was pure nonsense, of course, completely adrift from any Holy Authority and not at all what Boone was hoping for. Indeed, the Reverend H. James Lauderton had cobbled this gem together earlier in the morning from a fortune cookie—he had enjoyed a very satisfying Moo Goo Gai Pan Special at the House of the Chinese Moon near Brookhaven the night before—and the local weather forecast. With that admittedly thin *provenance,* even the Reverend sensed he had missed the mark and dialed it up.

"But you say, Brother, 'Why does he not?' Because the Lord was wit-ness between you and the wife of your youth, to whom you have been faithless. And let us prepare to rejoice and exalt and give Him Glory."

Boone just shook his head.

This was the kind of puzzling stuff the Reverend would often bring to the party, his shaky ministry—mobile, expedient, and creative—only loosely tethered to the conventions of the Faith. His pulls from the Good Book, and even the occasional gem from a Chinese fortune cookie, were random, never verbatim, and often nonsensical.

But the Reverend wasn't done. He glanced toward the gentle curve of the Mississippi not a mile away to the west, his smile tired but de-termined. *Good Lord,* he thought, *that kid on the weekend weather desk looked like he should've been home finishing his junior high science proj-ect. But damn if he wasn't right on the money. The storm's coming all right. Time to move this along, and close the deal.*

—※—

The Reverend—everyone knew this—had lost his parish years ago. It had served, if only thinly and briefly, to anchor a truer faith, the kind he had joyfully taken with him from his years at seminary. A parking de-cal from the Church of the Good Shepherd, faded away in the left corner of the back window of his pick-up, mocked his sad and tarnished jour-ney, and talk of an affair with a married parishioner trailed noisily be-hind him like a branch caught under the back bumper of his truck. His calling now was moved along less by the spirit of the Holy Ghost than the modest fees for his services—cash only please, gas money welcomed.

The Closer, the Reverend was called, although never to his face. He travelled the blue highways of the Deep South in search of redemption.

And those fees.

His only companions were Beau, two well-worn smudge-black suits, and the memories of his quiet parish along the coastal marshes of Carolina, just north of Beaufort.

But his easy forgiveness of the ways of the world, along with a kind of dusty charm and a charitable understanding of the tides of marriage, had earned him a certain circuit-riding fame across a dozen counties. And if his relationship to the Almighty was complicated (some would say *slippery*), he was the go-to guy for just this sort of tribal celebration of the serial-married, closing the deals the more buttoned-down local clergy shunned.

He was just what Boone needed, although at that moment Boone was not quite sure.

—⁂—

"Don't really know what you mean, Padre. I was hoping for a little more…"

The Closer looked up to the sky. *Skies really darkening now.* He then turned to the groom. "You need, maybe, some kind of *sign*?"

Boone just shrugged.

The Reverend again looked up, nudged Boone, closed his eyes, and appeared to pray. This traveling preacher had his shortcomings, but he certainly knew something about performance art, as well as the late afternoon summer weather in the Mississippi Delta.

KA-BOOM!

The lightning hit the water tower behind the house, skipping right over their heads and those of the startled guests. Most would later say they *felt* the whole thing an instant before the thunderclap, the acrid-electric smell slicing through the humid air. The wine glass pyramid crafted by the caterer's assistant—Katherine's young buck had been more than happy to help with the challenging engineering—crashed to the porch deck, and a loose board high atop the tower tumbled to the ground, narrowly missing a parked car.

A bit clichéd, The Closer thought, *but surely just what was needed.* With a wink he turned to Boone. "Looks like this *is* your lucky day. Let's do it."

—⁓—

The Closer stayed for just a few minutes of the reception, which spilled over the porch and on to the grounds where a tent had been set up. A small band had begun to play a confusing mix of songs, hoping to bridge the various generational divides among the younger guests of the bride—they were already doing some kind of line dance on the portable parquet floor in the center of the tent—and the older guests on Boone's team, who were mostly hanging around the bar on the porch. It promised to be a rather long evening and he had one more union to perform, a small ceremony over in Franklin County, just family.

He wrapped a couple of ham biscuits in a napkin and stuffed them into his pocket, where they joined his shirt button and an envelope with his fee. He wished the new couple the best, and quietly slipped away. As he buckled into his pick-up, he looked in his rearview mirror. This was habit, something he thought of as a kind of quiet benediction, the smile at the end of a job well done.

Just then the skies opened up, sheets of rain whipping through the live oaks, blowing horizontally in from the open sides of the tent and quickly finding a tear in the canvas directly above the drummer. He watched as everyone scrambled in full retreat, and he caught a last glimpse of Boone reaching for his bride to help her up the steps to the porch. Her dress was soaked, a muddy ring already circling the hem, her hair a soggy mess. Number Seven waved him off, stomping into the house. Boone started after her, then stopped, detouring instead over to the porch bar to join some of the older crowd.

There we go, The Closer thought, shaking his head.

He adjusted the mirror, and took the ham biscuits out of his pocket along with the envelope. He unfolded the napkin first, then rustled his dog awake to give him one of the biscuits. Opening the envelope, he smiled and turned to his traveling companion.

"And we got the gas money, too, Beau. *Praise the Lord.*"

The Man Inside

"He's in there, Father. This one's trouble, he is."

A plastic name badge pinned on his dark blue shirt suggested the guard's name was *R. Schmidt*, but there was loose talk that some of the officers at the Raymond D. Hopkins Correctional Center had started adopting a kind of stage name at work, building in a little extra distance between the men who would be going home after work and those who wouldn't.

Schmidt was not much older than the man standing next to him, Charlie O'Brien. Both were in their thirties, and both were staring into Cell B-16 at the man inside. The door, unlike most of those in the older prisons, was solid, with only a heavy glass slit about the size of a business envelope at eye level. Charlie's badge—not much smaller, and as white as his starched clerical collar—was clipped on the breast pocket of his blazer. It read, in bright red letters, *Visitor, B-Cell Only*.

A small sticker slapped on the lower corner read *October 29, 1992*.

He turned to Schmidt, and smiled. "Raised Catholic. Just a Low Episcopal now, Officer." Rarely did people call him Father. And if they did, he would nudge them back a notch with a wry smile. "Still kind of winging it." He paused. "Like most, I guess."

—⁂—

Until six weeks earlier, Charlie O'Brien hadn't been in a prison in over fifteen years, not since he wore a similar badge to visit his father, a hard-drinking and quick-tempered man working the oil rigs in the Gulf who was then doing time at a medium security prison outside Lafayette, Louisiana. And if you asked around certain parts of Southeast Texas, you would learn that Charlie had sometimes played it pretty tough too. Or at least until he left Port Arthur on a scholarship to Louisiana State. He was now an associate professor and chaplain at Southern Intermont College, a small private college tucked away in the foothills of the Blue Ridge Mountains, the crisp, clean air *good for the soul*, as he would often tell his students.

It had been for him. His wife, too.

Charlie usually taught two courses, *Religious Studies 221: Morality, Justice and Religious Thought,* and *Junior Seminar 412: The Old Testament.* However, weeks earlier the dean had suggested he drop *221,* a large lecture course, so that he could work the fall semester with Prison Outreach Ministries. He would need, the dean explained, to travel three days a week to a minimum-security facility upstate and once a week to the maximum-security Hopkins on Thursdays, but back in time to teach his seminar on Fridays.

Charlie knew that suggestions from the dean were always more than that, and agreed, if reluctantly. After that muddied start in East Texas he had learned to color within the lines, his attitude toward authority now *good.* He knew that for a fact because the state trooper who had recently written him up for speeding—*just nine miles-per-hour over,* Charlie had pleaded—had generously checked 'Attitude Good' in the box on the citation.

He'd kept it tucked away in his desk ever since.

Charlie was pleased that he didn't have to drop his Friday seminar where he did loosen things up a bit, *winging it* as he had just told Schmidt. He would circle high and more freely around the hard questions which the great minds have explored for centuries: whether justice can be distinguished from rightness, and whether it exists as an exclusive property of the legal institutional order only or as a derivative property of the individual as well. But Charlie also knew when to bring it all down, and he would talk about what he called "the guardrails." He would say they were there—like the sometimes-crumpled things to the sides of the tricky back roads all along the Blue Ridge—to keep things from simply spilling completely off the cliff.

The better students would forgive the tortured metaphor, especially in his mid-semester lecture on *The Laws of God and Man*. This lecture hinted at something else on the margin, something deep and important and personal.

The better students, although they would never know it, were right: Charlie had once thought of becoming a lawyer.

Then, in the spring of his second year at the Marshall Wythe School of Law at William & Mary, he dropped out, enrolling at Virginia Theological the following fall. He rarely talked about that sudden change, other than to say he simply decided to put his faith in a power higher than the Code of the Commonwealth of Virginia. Sometimes he would add that for him it was simply the right choice at the right time, as was his decision to go to Southern Intermont. And to those who knew Charlie well it was clear he and his wife had found a home at Intermont, although she could see Charlie was finding his work with Prison Outreach difficult.

She also knew why.

And years later, when Charlie would think of Officer R. Schmidt and the Raymond D. Hopkins Correctional Center and the man inside cell B-16 on that crusty October day in the fall of 1992, he would try to remember only the gray nothingness of the day, and the dance of the huge red-tailed hawk, and the tiny barn swallow with the broken wing.

Not how the man inside the tiny cell had seemed *so fucking pleased with himself*.

—⚉—

Charlie had begun his day at the prison with a Christian-Interfaith group meeting in A-Building, heavy on the lessons of *Ephesians 4.1-6* and capped with an earnest, if ragged, singing of *For Freedom Christ Has Set Us Free!* The tougher part of his job, counseling the B-Building prisoners in their own cells, had taken up the afternoon. It had been, as Charlie always expected, another long Thursday, and B-16 was the last of his six cell ministries.

Schmidt paused in front of the cell. "Tellin' ya, this one's a real prince. Nothin' but trouble."

Charlie wasn't yet quite sure what to make of Schmidt, even after a long day together.

Earlier, while they finished a quick lunch in the staff canteen, the guard had tried to hand Charlie six thick and well-worn summaries of the criminal and institutional record of each inmate on his afternoon rounds. Charlie told him to hang on to them, at least until the end of the day, adding that he tried to look at the prisoners' current spiritual needs rather than their past bad acts. Politely, he thought, although Schmidt had looked annoyed.

But Charlie also sensed that Schmidt had a well-practiced sense of what went on around Hopkins.

And a little caution, after a long day, was not a bad idea.

"Trouble?"

The guard nodded. "I mean, this guy's in and out of C-Unit Isolation so often they ought to charge him rent over there." He shook his head. "Something wrong with this one, there is. Deep inside, you know. I can feel these things, after sixteen years around here. *Evil*, that's what's in this one." Schmidt moved to open the cell, then stopped. "Word around here is he lawyered up good, some fancy attorney winding a jury so tight with some cooked-up defense that they never saw it, that evil. Me, I don't much care about the finer points of the law. Guys like this should be sent for a squat on Old Sparky. That simple, at least it is for me."

Charlie knew all about Old Sparky, the electric chair which once sat in Richmond at the old State Penitentiary on Spring Street, executions now carried out in Jarratt. A while back one went very wrong, the whole thing a terrible mess. He and his wife sometimes talked about it, mostly late at night, with the call for abolishing the death penalty growing loud.

"Carved up a college girl. Maybe six years ago, near the Naval Weapons Depot in Yorktown. That's what Johnny Kremmer did."

Shit.

—⁊⁊—

Charlie O'Brien, in his second year at William & Mary, took the narrow stairs to Stephanie Braydon's apartment on the second floor of a two-bedroom carriage house close to campus that she shared with two other girls. It was just before 4:30 in the morning, dark except for the lights in the living room. And what Charlie would always remember about that night in the spring of 1986 was how those lights shone out on some wisteria—bright, beautiful living things—crawling up the broken trellis under the window of the bedroom Lauren Gardella shared with his girlfriend Stephanie Braydon, across the hall from Beth Jenkins.

Nothing good happens after midnight, his mother used to tell him.

His mother was right.

Less than twenty minutes earlier, Beth Jenkins had called Charlie at his apartment three blocks away to tell him that Lauren Gardella had been found, her body in the heavy brush near one of the historical marker turn-offs on the Colonial Parkway. It was a secluded spot, a nice place not six miles away to watch the small boats on the York River during the day and the moon over the river at night.

Lauren Gardella had been missing for three days.

She had last been seen heading out after her Saturday lunch shift at the Broken Crust, a popular pizza place near campus, with a guy who had been hanging around the place for a couple of months, a regular who often came in for lunch with a couple buddies, and sometimes alone.

Beth was sitting on the small second-hand living room sofa, a counselor from student health sitting in a chair next to her. Charlie looked towards Stephanie's bedroom, the door closed. "She just went in to call Lauren's brother. Why don't you give her…"

Charlie nodded.

"It's all a nightmare, Charlie. I'm tiptoeing around in a fog. This shit just doesn't happen, not around here."

Beth Jenkins, Stephanie Braydon and Lauren Gardella had roomed together on campus for three years, all working a few lunch shifts a week to afford the carriage house for their last year.

It would be, they promised each other, their best.

Beth had always been the calm in any storm, a no-nonsense pre-med who had just gotten accepted at the Medical College of Virginia. She also worked one weekend a month at the MCV Hospital in Richmond. And if she seemed to be holding it together, her eyes—red and pleading—told a different story.

"*Why?*" Beth pulled a blanket up to her chin, and looked at Charlie. "They got someone in custody, been coming into The Broken Crust regularly, for what, a couple months? Lunch maybe three times a week, along with a few other guys working that construction project down the block, all a little older than our college crowd, but none of them seeming, like, whacked, no sirens going off. And shit," she winced, nodding toward the counselor, "I work psych at MCV Saturday nights."

Beth looked away. "All of them just chatting us up, the usual nonsense. Mostly funny stuff, nothing crazy." She paused. "Heard him once say he wouldn't be doing any of the heavy work on the site for a good while, something about messing up his back in the service then popping something a few weeks ago. Other guys giving him a rough time, you know. Maybe that's why he always seemed to be fishing around a little harder for a date, something about a boat over on the York." Beth hesitated. "*All* of us he was pushing, Charlie. Even Stephanie. But she chilled him off quick, told him she was allergic to water." Beth nodded towards Stephanie's bedroom. "You know she pulls that brush-off all the time. Everyone gets it, even the losers, and she never sinks a tip. But Steph told me how pissed he looked, something..." Beth paused. "It scared her a bit. And now I'm thinking maybe I should have seen—"

Beth hesitated, and Charlie knew then that all of them would be broken in one way or another, and that this night would never end. "But not Lauren. Told us, what, it's now six days ago, she thought he was cute, kind of fun. And since *she* was not allergic to water, she was going out on his boat—not really a date, she said, just a Saturday afternoon spin on the river with a few of the other guys from the crew, maybe catch a few beers after—"

Charlie looked away, then started toward Stephanie's bedroom door, the one she had shared with Lauren Gardella for their best year ever.

"She fought back, Charlie. I know she did. Real hard."

—⁓—

The Commonwealth of Virginia v. Johnny Langston Kremmer, Criminal Docket Number CR-86-312, played out over the third week of May in 1986, in Courtroom 4 on the second floor of the old Criminal Courts Building in Williamsburg, the Honorable P. Reno Miller presiding.

Skipping his law classes, Charlie O'Brien was there every day, getting a less sanitized lesson in the law.

The prosecution argued that Johnny Kremmer's brutal stabbing of Lauren Simpson Gardella along the Colonial Parkway on the night of April 3rd was willful, deliberate and premeditated—in the mind of the jurors, they hoped, a bloody murder of the coldest sort—meeting its statutory burden to prove he committed the crime of first-degree murder, a Class 2 felony.

The lawyered-up, thick alphabet soup of a "diminished capacity" defense that played out over several days boiled down to this: the prosecution had failed to carry its burden of proving intent. Johnny Kremmer, they argued, had that day taken a new medication prescribed by his doctor at the VA over in Norfolk for an injury "suffered in the service of his country." That, in combination with another prescribed drug he was taking for something called "mild personality fragmentation," triggered in the defendant what one psychiatrist called an "involuntary"—*objection*—"hallucinatory fugue" at the time he killed Lauren Gardella. In a "dissociative state," Johnny Kremmer's capacity to understand what he was doing, the defense argued, had diminished *to the vanishing point.*

Charlie O'Brien would look at the jury, trying to see if they could make sense out of any of it.

He didn't think they could.

For each of those long days, as witnesses were examined and crossed, the case seemingly going one way and then another, Charlie would wonder where the soft smile of Lauren Gardella, the sobbing nightmares of Stephanie Braydon, and the wounded strength of Beth Jenkins fit into the whole thing.

And on the last day of the trial the defense argued that no jury, under the facts before them, could find the defendant guilty of murder in the first degree.

And this one didn't.

After three days of deliberation, marked by a flurry of confusing questions to the court, the jury delivered its verdict of manslaughter, a crime carrying a minimum sentence of only five years. The press screamed that he had, literally, gotten away with murder, and Johnny Kremmer soon began to serve his sentence of seven years imprisonment at the Raymond D. Hopkins Correctional Center.

Charlie O'Brien never returned to the study of law, leaving William & Mary three weeks later.

—⁓—

"You okay?"

"Just let me in."

"You don't look so—"

"*In,* Officer Schmidt."

The guard started to open the cell, and he could see Johnny Kremmer lazily sitting on his bunk. Very little light shone through the narrow cell window, high up, the inky gray nothingness of the day outside seeping into Cell B-16. Schmidt turned to Charlie. "You sure you—?"

"*Fucking right I'm sure.*"

Schmidt opened the cell.

The man inside, Charlie could see, was thinner than he remembered the last he saw him.

That was almost six years ago, in Courtroom 4 on the second floor of the Criminal Courts Building in Williamsburg, Virginia, the Honorable. P. Reno Miller presiding.

—⁂—

"Stand up." Charlie's words were hard, and sharp.

"What?" Johnny Kremmer looked confused.

"Stand up." Charlie took a step toward the prisoner. "You heard me."

The guard, monitoring things inside, heard nothing of this, although he would say later that he saw a puzzled look on Kremmer's face.

"Come on, man. Chill. You're supposed to be my—"

"I'm your fucking *nothing.*" Charlie was losing it, things buried exploding deep inside, emotional guard-rails peeling away with a savagery which mocked his calling.

It terrified him.

The sins of the father.

But he did not—could not—stop. "Nothing but a friend of *Lauren Gardella.* A very, very good friend," Charlie took another step forward. "And Lauren was the roommate of Stephanie Braydon, my girlfriend when I was at William & Mary." Charlie paused. "I sat in the back of that fucking courtroom every day."

Charlie—he knows this now and always has—could have dialed it down at that, waving a back hand to the guard to let him out and calling it a day. A long day. But it didn't play out that way, things unwinding as they do, even for the good ones.

Johnny Kremmer's smirk broadened to a toothy grin. "Yeah, I remember Stephanie. Worked the Broken Crust too. Quite a looker, man. A mouthy thing, she was. Guess you're just lucky it wasn't—"

Charlie O'Brien ripped off his collar and lunged toward Johnny Kremmer.

He didn't get there.

Schmidt rushed in, wrapping Charlie in a bear lock. He dragged him out of the cell and locked the door quickly.

Schmidt shook his head. "I've pulled three or four *lawyers* out of cells over the years, but nothing like *this*."

Charlie knew he'd already broken through the guard-rails. "That girl? That *college girl*? Her name was Lauren Gardella." He choked. "I knew her well, when I was at William & Mary Law. She was—" Charlie wheeled around when he saw Schmidt drop his jaw: Kremmer had picked up Charlie's collar and was sporting it around his neck, a mocking grin on his face.

"Give me those keys, Schmidt."

Schmidt looked at Charlie, then through the window at Johnny Kremmer. "You know I can't do that." They both stood in silence before the guard turned back to Charlie. "But maybe…" Schmidt stopped. "I mean, I can get your collar."

Charlie hesitated, the silence long and awkward. "No… no. Let's just get out of here." He sighed. "I guess you're going to have to write this up?"

Schmidt shrugged. "Don't worry about it. Things happen around here. No one got hurt, long day. Let's just call it a little misunderstanding." Schmidt paused. "He'll make a stink, but…"

Charlie nodded. "Yeah. A long day."

The two of them walked slowly out of B-Building, toward the admin office. Things were quiet, no one around, when Schmidt turned to Charlie.

"Had to be rough, back then, for you."

"You have no idea. We were broken, all of us. I tried—I'm still trying—to pick up the pieces with—" He reached for his collar, then shrugged when his hand came up empty "Well, I've tried to make a difference. Faith helps, you know." Charlie shook his head. "Only a few folks know I didn't want to get into this Prison Outreach thing. Even fewer know why." Charlie looked at Schmidt. "Pretty much just you now, and my wife. Stephanie."

"From…"

"Yeah. Can we keep it that way?"

Schmidt nodded. "Sure. Best for everybody." He hesitated, then opened Kremmer's official file and flipped through a couple of pages. "Yeah, just what I thought. He's coming up for release in less than a year." Schmidt shook his head. "Sixteen years on the job around here, I sometimes wonder about the whole point." He paused. "You know, I got a cousin over at Intermont, Randi Phinney. Nice girl, a senior. Told me she took your seminar on the Old Testament last year."

Charlie O'Brien remembered her, an earnest student who had a little trouble with the final.

"Did she like it?"

"Liked it fine, but thought your exam was a little tough."

"They say that a lot." Charlie smiled, although not broadly, for the first time that day. "A couple students complain every year that I can get a little, well, *salty*, too. Guess you could figure that after…" He nodded back toward B-Building. "Maybe when you file your report you can scrub some of the… salt?"

"Sure." Schmidt shrugged, then looked at Charlie. "Bet I'd like that seminar of yours too, being kind of an Old Testament guy myself." He looked around. "*An eye for an eye*, that's what I say." Schmidt dropped his voice, and looked Charlie hard in the eye. "Blue Ridge justice. You know."

Just then a small bird, maybe a barn swallow, swooped low over the far wall of the prison, chasing a much larger red-tailed hawk. But the smaller bird's wing appeared damaged, its flight jerky, the larger bird suddenly pulling up and turning on the crippled bird. Both men winced.

"You see that, Officer Schmidt?"

Schmidt nodded.

"Not a fair fight." Charlie said, feeling again for his lost collar. "Maybe nothing ever really is." The two men stared in silence as the big hawk, with the crippled bird screeching in its talons, began to circle over the prison grounds. The hawk's flight was wide and lazy and, Charlie thought, somehow *obscene.*

Officer Schmidt broke the silence. "Like I said before, things happen around here."

—⚉—

Charlie knows now, as he knew deep inside then, what Officer Schmidt was saying, and how to respond.

Gestures and words of the simplest sort come easily to mind.

And as he closes his eyes and thinks of the cold gray nothingness of that day in 1992, Charlie sometimes hears—*so clearly*—those words of the simplest sort, *his own words,* cutting through the light chill of that day, along with the cries of the helpless smaller bird falling, falling…

She fought back, Charlie. Real hard.

On those other occasions—those other times when he closes his eyes and feels those words of the simplest sort dissolve on the tip of his tongue before they could cut into the gray of that day—Charlie sees nothing but the hint of a nod from Officer R. Schmidt, the guard's eyes glancing over to B-Building.

NO! I've got it wrong. There was nothing in that. Nothing there. Surely. Unless…

NO!

—⚉—

Charlie O'Brien never again set foot in the Raymond D. Hopkins Correctional Center. Or any other prison either, resigning from the Prison Outreach Ministry on Monday morning.

No one got hurt, R. Schmidt said.

Charlie O'Brien knew differently.

Sometimes, even years later in the deep marrow of a cold Blue Ridge winter's night, Stephanie would feel Charlie thrash about. She knew to always wake him, and why. She would stroke his thinning hair, and they would talk about those things which begin as a slow slide to the margins of anyone's life, hovering at the edge of an abyss. These are the worrisome things, things that get hard stuck to the edges.

He would then ask Stephanie to tell him a story about Lauren Gardella. A nice story, he would say. She would always do just that, in a soft whisper, until Charlie O'Brien, a man who circled the hard questions at a small college in the foothills of the Blue Ridge, drifted back to sleep.

Bump O'Rourke

I was early for my meeting in Bellows Corner, a dot on the map which hugs a tired branch of the Connecticut River about a two-hour drive from Boston.

My job is a sad one, and tedious. It takes me to the many forgotten factory towns along the river. And that day I would be talking to the owners of the Two Tap, a quiet tavern along the town's now-abandoned branch siding of the Boston & Maine Railroad. A hard-working couple had bought the place a few years ago as a retirement investment, but that was not working out so well. I dreaded a morning of tough conversations about debt ratios and cash flow and the many treacheries of what was left of the economy after the whole thing tanked a decade ago.

That's just the thing: I rarely get to deliver good news, and I knew that I wouldn't that day. The Two Tap was running out of cash, and the Boston Bank & Trust Company was running out of patience.

I had some time to swing over by the river, so I did. I passed old textile mills and factories that were shuttered and overgrown, their deaths occasioned by cheap foreign labor and mostly un-mourned by anything more than rusty *For Sale* signs. A couple had been *repurposed*, as they say, from their former glory, one now a funky metal-art gallery, another some kind of technical school. Further along was the shell of another factory, its chimney charred but still mostly standing as chimneys all seem to do after a fire. Faded white letters ran vertically down the brown-red brick, telling anyone who cared that it had once been the Edgar Ball-Bearing Company.

A chain-link fence surrounded the property, and in front of it was one of those heavy iron historical markers that dot the backroads all over New England. They have become something of a hobby for me, a way to break up my time on the road. I pulled off, and got out of the car.

Sometimes the markers jog at least a passing memory of a history I had once studied, history writ large: of battles won, heroes born, sacrifices noble and daring and important. But other times they share the lesser stories, and these are often the sad ones I have come to think of as *footnote tragedies*.

This was one of those.

It told of an explosion and fire at the ball-bearing factory on June 23, 1937, destroying the building and taking the lives of fourteen workers as well as three volunteer firemen from Woonsocket. They are, it said, all buried together in a special section of the town cemetery, honored on a monument dedicated a year later. It seemed right that at least the tragic death of these workers, and the company itself, would not go unremembered.

I got back into my car and headed to my bank's branch office in town just a block away from the Two Tap to do my job.

The meeting was short, but strained, and I needed a beer afterwards. And I knew only too well that the place could use the business.

—᙮᙮—

I walked the block—the light chill earlier that May morning had lifted—and entered the tavern. Like so many in the old factory towns—maybe it had something to do with the smudgy small-paned windows, or the beamed wood ceiling—it was dark, but not unpleasantly so. Table lamps and shaded lighting hung from the ceiling doing their quiet jobs, the neon beer signs behind the bar pushing for the more dramatic. It had nothing of the phony feel of the chains and tourist places over on the Cape—places, at least to me, always seeming to try too hard—and I liked the place immediately, which didn't help my mood.

My boss—he hasn't been on the road for years—tells me to always look at my job as *just business,* but it never is.

The next thing I noticed, other than the place seemed empty, were the dozens of framed photos covering the walls, mostly of baseball players. They commanded a closer look, a pull that nothing hanging on an Applebee's could ever hope to match. Many were faded black and white photos of entire teams; others individual players in striped knee britches and caps, out-sized moustaches, tough guys in baggy shirts with *Bellows Corner* stitched across the chest in a graceful old-style script, like you might see on a vintage circus wagon. Others looked newer, a few in color with *Bellows Corner* a rich scarlet on a light gray baseball blouse, the hats also scarlet with a bold *BC* on the crown.

Tacked up behind the bar was a large dark blue pennant with *Champs, 1921-23, 1927,* in white, and a smaller one with *Champs, 1935,* in red. A curious stain crept along the left border of the small banner, looking like a fat potato, splotchy and mottled brown. A few more team pennants were scattered about the place, including the obligatory one for the Red Sox and another smaller one for the Yankees that had been roundly defaced and apparently shot with a small-bore rifle.

I sat down at the bar on a high-backed stool. No one else in sight, I wasn't so sure that cold beer was in my near future. I studied the fat potato for a minute, then swiveled around to take in the photos in wide-angle. I couldn't shake the sense, the pleasant sense, that I just *belonged* there.

"You like baseball?"

I turned back around to see a guy walking out of the kitchen in back, behind the bar. He was carrying a case of Narragansett beer, which he set down on the low back counter. "You bet. That and a cold beer on a warming day. Those Narragansetts cold?"

He nodded, then pulled a dark green bottle from the chiller and placed it carefully on a scuffed and stained coaster which looked like a flattened baseball, although the printed seam stitches were comically oversized. *Probably made in China,* I thought, *like most things these days.* "Bump O'Rourke," he said, sticking out his paw which was about the size of a waffle griddle, and scarred. Fit, early forties I guessed. Hard to tell in these old factory towns.

"Pete. Pete MacGregor," I said, my mood continuing to lift with his broad grin and his firm grip.

He was wearing a sun-faded baseball cap, worn thin on the brim like an old tire. His shirt was long-sleeved denim, his trousers a pair of wrinkled khakis. His eyes were friendly, but he seemed to hold something back, and I guessed he took me for the banker I am, or at least a city-boy—my dark gray suit and Vineyard Vines tie the easy money bet. I took a long draw on my beer, then pointed to the walls, fishing for a little common ground.

"Did you ever play?"

Bump smiled. "Sure did. Outfield, mostly in right. I first suited up around here when the team was sponsored by the Edgar Ball-Bearing Company, part of the original Federation."

"Federation?"

"Teams from the mill towns. We played for the love of the game." He winked. "Well, maybe a little for the ladies too, coming over from Fall River. Called them the *Fall River Debs.*"

Bump seemed to be enjoying this, his *rivah* a happy reminder of the Boston "*r*" dropped along with the tea into the harbor long ago. "I wasn't much of a fielder, but that soon didn't matter. I was a steady hitter, mostly spraying singles into short left. Fast around the bases too, before the knees went. Then I moved on to coaching third until I took over managing the boys, not long after the Two Tap started sponsoring the team."

"So you're still…"

"In the game?" He smiled. "Oh yeah. We all are." He pointed to a few guys playing pool in the back room I hadn't noticed before. "Let me show you something." Bump pulled a piece of paper from his wallet and carefully unfolded it. "Here's the line-up for Saturday. I'm thinking of making some changes." He laughed. "Some of the boys won't be happy, you know." He put the paper back in his wallet. "How about you, Pete. You ever play?"

I don't get that question much anymore, so I jumped right in. "I walked on at Furman, an accounting major with a fair arm. Had a couple good years at the plate, too." I took another draw of my beer. "Shuffled around the infield, wound up at first for my last two years. Hung it up after my senior year."

"But you caught the magic…" Bump looked at me hard, winked, then pointed to a large photo just to the side of the door. "I think you might like that photo over there." He smiled. "Go ahead, take a look."

I walked over to the photo, about the size of an old *Life* magazine, matted and framed. A player was leaning on an oversized bat, his uniform fresh, the photo clearly staged to catch the *Edgar Ball-Bearing Company* ad on the outfield fence. He looked like a younger version of the guy behind the bar, but without the cares that I sensed he carried. A caption, in large capital letters, read:

JACKSON "BUMP" O'ROURKE

In smaller letters, centered under his name on a polished brass plate screwed to the frame:

1919 Rookie of the Year

I'm a numbers guy, and something was off here. *Way off.* I turned around.

"Bump, that caption…" I was fumbling around.

Bump seemed ready for this. "I was just a kid, right out of college. Worcester Tech."

"But…"

Bump nodded to the clock over the bar. "We love baseball because we all know this: the game lives *outside time.*" He paused. "So many other things tied to the clock, you know, ticking down to… *what?*" He smiled. "Jobs, most of our sports, or at least the ones we care about around here. Football, basketball, hockey. All tied to the countdown, the clock. Always the clock. *You can lose to the clock,* that's what the coaches all say. But not baseball." Bump paused, then looked at me. "You ever hear of a guy named Roger Angell?"

"Sure, the great baseball writer…"

"That's right. He talked about the ballpark as a special place where time itself moves differently—seamless, invisible, a bubble. Magic, if you want to call it that. A place marked by no clock, just the breaks of the game, time measured in nothing more than outs. He made it all sound so simple: all you have to do is keep hitting, keep the rally going, and you have *defeated time.* You can go on *forever.* No one's ever said it better, although they all try."

Bump took a damp rag to a spot on the old mahogany bar. "We're the forgotten folks around here, but we've found our way to beat time, me and the boys, to stop the clock. That's the real promise of the game of baseball. And it's *ours.*" I heard a weariness in his voice. "But here's the thing, Pete. The game can also break your heart." His voice barely above a whisper, his eyes focused somewhere far away, he shook his head, sadly, and he suddenly looked older. "I love the game, always have, but sometimes I just wish the whole thing…" He stopped, then pulled absently at a loose thread on the brim of his hat. "Magic? A miracle?" He paused. "Our redemption, our—my—salvation? Or is it a… is it something else, something darker? No one knows."

"Bump, I'm trying to…"

Bump leaned forward. "Just let it in, Pete. It's what I've learned to do." He looked toward the boys in the back. "It all started in the summer of 1937, first time we played after the big fire at the ball-bearing factory." Bump paused. "Game between Bellows Corner and the Woonsocket Zephyrs. They were mostly mill guys like us, a team sponsored by Worthington Amalgamated Industries, although they stuffed their bench with younger kids from their volunteer fire department." He paused. "Fine boys, and they had lost a couple of their own in the fire, too. So we let it go, both teams trying to soldier on for the guys we lost, the rest of us looking for something, anything to keep us going. Game started about two on a Saturday afternoon without a cloud in the sky, their home field."

Bump closed his eyes, just for a moment. He seemed to glide away, somewhere.

"Game scoreless until an error by their shortstop in the top of the seventh puts one of our guys on first, with two outs. Our catcher, a burly pipefitter on the line named McDuffey—a real screw-up everywhere but the ballpark—takes a couple called strikes before he pockets one into the left-center bleachers." Bump paused. "He had been backing-up our regular catcher, Bus Torrington, who died in the fire." Bump smiled. "Bus was such a good kid, special. Married my cousin, he did. Left a cute little boy at home."

He flipped a rag over his shoulder. "Woonsocket blows a couple chances in the bottom of the eighth, leaving runners on first and second. We open the top of the ninth up by two, with our three best hitters up—Kowalski, Marcella, and Allen. Kowalski catches a slider on the outside corner, sending a sizzler right past the second baseman. Marcella takes a called strike on the first pitch, then powders a line drive into short center, driving Kowalski to third. Johnny Allen, a tall Irishman from the Bronx, parks his first pitch, a slider that forgets to slide, into the bleachers, dead center."

Bump fiddled with that loose thread on his hat.

"Pete, here's the thing. We just *couldn't stop hitting*. Naughten— a new kid who'd just replaced a hard-drinking welder from Swampscott named Muldoon, who..." Bump seemed to stumble. "Well, Pops Naughten bloops a cheap single, Ducky Murrell doubles on a full count, and Marty Incadela taps a slow roller past the pitcher. We're hitting everything coming our way, runs piling up like a bad debt. We run the order." Bump smiled. "Then we run it again. The inning, *our glorious Bellows Corner inning*, just wouldn't end. The game stretches into the near darkness. No lights, you know."

Bump chuckled, his eyes seeming to refocus. "We *owned* the top of the ninth, Pete, the Zephyrs running out of pitchers, the day running out of light. The ump wanted to call it, but Woonsocket demanded the game resume the next Saturday, hoping for their chance to break the rally and get their last turn at the bat."

"Kind of a long-shot, down, what, seventeen runs?" I've heard crazier stories across my polished desk in downtown Boston, so I went along.

"*Nineteen* really, but they made their point." Bump looked around, taking in the photos. "So we resumed play here the next week, but Woonsocket never got to their bottom of the ninth." Bump smiled. "Not that Saturday. Not the next Saturday. *Not any other Saturday since.* It's been over eighty years now, what we call *The Rally* around here, at least me and the boys, and I owe it to them." Bump shrugged, "*All of them*, Pete." He nodded in the direction of the back room. "It was that promise of *forever*, the promise of all the ballparks, you know." He took a minute, then continued. "Just look around this town, Pete. It's all that keeps us going." He looked me hard in the eye. "That, and this place." He paused again. "We're playing Saturday. You should come."

I liked this guy, but you should know this. I come from old Georgia stock, steeped in the colorful legends and lore which live in the dusty places in towns along the rivers and among moss-draped oaks throughout the Old South. These are the places where a tall tale is as likely to be served up as shrimp and grits to those traveling through, and always to the tourists from New Jersey. Indeed, I spent one summer during college giving those cooked-up evening carriage tours through the spookier parts of Savannah, and then another in Beaufort, the kind with things both seen and unseen in the shadows, heaping nonsense on top of nonsense in the cause of the tourist dollar, and I sensed I was being played. But it was not, I felt, with malice, and at least I hadn't been thinking about debt ratios for some time.

"No, don't think I can make it, Bump." I fibbed about some other plans, the easy out which I hoped suggested I had gotten the play, no hard feelings.

Sometimes we just do what we do, but I think I really just didn't want to mess with a guy having a little fun with the city boy, or maybe I was feeling guilty about the hammer I was about to drop on the Tap. Or maybe—just maybe—I needed to think there really is a little magic left in our world, and I didn't want to see the man behind the curtain.

No one does.

We chatted a little longer, pleasantly, about nothing really. I finished my beer, said goodbye, and headed home to Boston.

Over the next few weeks I thought how good a cold beer can taste at the end of a bad day at work, not only for tired bankers traveling through but for the good people in the forgotten towns who deserved better. But mostly I thought about what smart college boys who are good with numbers sometimes need to do.

Cash flow is not magic, you know, and a job is just a job.

I had a few ideas, and caught my boss before he decamped for a long weekend on the Cape. I figured he would be in a good mood, and that the new numbers I had polished for the owners of the Two Tap would pass corporate muster.

I was right.

Not long after, maybe two months, I read a brief back-pages story in *The Globe* that the old ball field in Bellows Corner had been destroyed by fire, the regular Saturday industrial league game "*postponed indefinitely.*"

A few weeks later I drove back to the town, directly to the Two Tap. I hoped I might find Bump behind the bar, and learn a little more about what happened. But the bartender was just a kid, a scarlet baseball hat loose on his head, the brim flat like they all wear them today.

At least it wasn't on backwards. I settled into a stool at the bar and ordered a beer. "From the chiller, please," I added, just because I can sometimes be a jerk.

The kid nodded, and plopped a familiar green bottle on one of those smudged baseball coasters. The place, I was happy to see, seemed pleasantly busy, a younger crowd sitting around some new tables in the back room where the pool table had been.

"Bump O'Rourke around?" I asked.

The bartender hesitated. "You mean *Jimmy* O'Rourke?"

"No. *Bump* O'Rourke, first name *Jackson*. He served me a beer a couple months ago. That man could talk baseball, about his team of tough mill guys with names like Muldoon and Naughten and Kowalski and Marcella, some Irishman from the Bronx named Allen. Spun a good yarn, too, something about a rally. Tried to wheel me right in, he did." I pointed to Bump's picture on the wall. It hadn't moved.

The kid looked puzzled "Mister... he's... he's dead. Died a few weeks ago."

He pointed to a framed newspaper clipping on the far wall. "Just after the ballfield fire in town. Folks say he walked over to the field the day after and collapsed near the dugout, or what was left of it. And here's the thing." The kid slowed down. "Story goes that in the factory fire in '37, *the big fire,* Bump O'Rourke barely got out after the first explosion, pulling along some kid named Bus Torrington, but the kid died a couple days later. Bump tried to go back in to save others; then the floor collapsed. He was burned, mostly on his hands. Lucky, I guess, although he took it all hard." The kid paused again. "You see, it was the second shift, Bump's shift, and he was in charge. No one really knows what happened, although there was talk that a welder on the shift, some guy named Muldoon, had been drinking." The kid shook his head. "They say Bump blamed himself for letting the welder take the floor that day."

The kid measured his speech. "Muldoon never made it out... justice, I guess. But nothing right about the other boys up there on the walls who were lost in the collapse too." The kid shook his head. "The ball-bearing factory never re-opened, most of the guys who survived finding other jobs in the mills around town. Times around here were better then, I guess, even in the Depression. But Bump O'Rourke never again set foot in another factory. At least that's what they say. Bump even owned this place for a few years, with a little help from the old Savings & Thrift, his wife working behind the bar most weekends. At least until just before she died in the late fifties." The kid smiled. "Quite a looker, that's what I hear, a gal from Fall River."

I remembered Bump's nod to the *Debs*.

He pointed to a far wall. "We just put up that local clipping about the ballpark fire, along with a couple photos of the crowd gathered for Bump's funeral." The kid frowned. "Some teenagers broke into the old ballfield's press box, and were just fooling around, smoking they say. The old place was tinder, kids lucky to get out." He looked over to the wall. "One of them was Bus Torrington's great grandson. Go figure." He paused again. "Of course, kids been doing that for decades, you know, and folks been warning them forever that they shouldn't." He shrugged. "Time just caught up, I guess."

I walked over to take a look. The floor creaked—*of course it did*— and I suddenly thought of Bump's faith in forever, which I guess is just the stuff of dreams, and maybe kids in a dusty press box on a warm evening, after all.

"Town got together and decided to add Bump's marker at the monument honoring the *Bellows Corner* boys lost in the 1937 fire, along with... Well, you'll see. I went out there with my girlfriend just the other day. The grounds are pretty overgrown, everywhere else most of the headstones are tilted, some barely standing in broken formation. My girlfriend said they looked like exhausted soldiers." He paused. "I don't know. But here's the strange thing: the monument's made out of brick from the old factory, and I swear it has the fire-damaged smell of, well... death. But I know that really can't be, you know, after all these years."

"No," I said quietly. "It probably can't."

"Hey, if you want to see for yourself, the cemetery is just past the old factories and the ballpark. The ruins of the ballpark, I guess I should say now." He turned to draw a beer for someone else, then looked back to me. "They take pretty good care of that section of the cemetery." He paused. "You want another one?"

"No. No, I don't think so."

I sat there for a few moments, finishing my beer. I then took a ten out of my wallet and left it on the bar top.

As I turned to leave, the kid stopped me.

"Say, mister, you the guy from Boston Bank & Trust?"

I nodded.

The kid touched the brim of his cap with two fingers, and handed me back my money.

"Thanks, and the beer's on the house." He smiled. "This place means everything to us, you know."

I did.

—⁓—

I could have headed straight back to Boston, grabbed a couple pops at the bar near where I live—the one that people think is the real Cheers but isn't, its own little inside joke—and crafted for my buddies, in my best good ole Georgia boy way, a crazy little story about one Mr. Jackson "Bump" O'Rourke. Just let the whole thing go, you know, but giving due to a town that could spin a tall tale across the generations—flawlessly, as far as I could tell, with everyone but the outsiders clued in.

But I drove over to the cemetery instead.

I parked the car under the shade of a full-bodied maple near the wrought-iron entrance gate, which was ajar. I sat there for a few minutes, watching a groundskeeper in a far corner wrestle with some old headstone that did indeed look like a tired soldier who had slipped out of formation. I got out of the car, and entered the cemetery. The grounds were less hallowed than overgrown, and it wasn't hard to see a patch in better shape, a small monument standing sentinel.

I threaded my way over there, stepping gently. The monument, shoulder-high and tapered towards the top, was made of old brick. It certainly did look like old brick from the ball-bearing factory, and it had the fire-damaged smell of tragedy like the kid had said, although the breeze was blowing directly over from the ballfield ruined by its own fire.

A brass plaque, centered on the top of the monument, seemed freshly polished. I leaned in for a closer look.

Lost
in The Great Edgar Ball-Bearing Company Fire
of June 23, 1937

In front of the monument rested several headstones, really just simple granite markers in a neat row. Most were faded, the engravings shallow and weathered, but I could make out a couple—Bus Torrington and Sean Muldoon.

And just below were two rows of obviously new markers, their granite polished, the engraved dates of their birth and death crisp, the dirt fresh. I leaned in for a closer look. I'm a numbers guy, remember, a banker in dark gray suits and starchy shirts and preppy ties, and I'm not prone to—well, this is the thing: each of them had left this world within a couple days of the ballpark fire in June.

The youngest, Eddie "The Hammer" Marcella, was, by the simple math of the granite marker, not quite 117. Most of the others—I recognized Allen, Kowalski, and McDuffey the pipefitter—were well into their 120's. I bent down to brush a little dirt off the marker I had really come to see:

Jackson "Bump" O'Rourke
February 16, 1897- June 17, 2019

—⁓—

We all see what we see, and believe what we believe. As for me, I'm just a tired banker who's good with numbers and played the great game of baseball a long time ago, and at least once found a way to do a little good in a world that could use a lot more, no matter what inning, and no matter who's up.

A Lovely Evening,
All Things Considered

—⁓—

To hear Randy tell the story, it was never really about the dinner with the Pritchards at all. It was simply the cosmic cruelty of the *Lutz Equation* at work, although the sauteed pork medallions certainly played a part—he will concede this, but only after a few beers—and the contractor too.

—⁂—

The dinner had been Gillian Hall's idea, Dan and Sharon Pritchard the full measure of idealized domesticity. Their four-bedroom clapboard colonial at 219 Windermere Lane, a quiet street lined with tall bur oaks, middling ambitions, and short mailboxes in a tony suburb of Kansas City, spoke of nothing less than the Great American Dream. Or at least that of the conventional sort: a loving marriage, good jobs, a couple kids, a dog, a fifteen-year fixed mortgage with no prepayment penalty, and a household debt-to-income ratio under twenty-nine percent.

But to Gillian, back in a cramped apartment she shared with two other teachers in a decidedly un-leafy corner of Philadelphia, that clapboard colonial—and the treasures of the marital good life that flowed throughout the Pritchard franchise like a mid-priced and not too oaky domestic wine—promised even more. It was the perfect setting to nudge her boyfriend Tripp Whitley off his sorry ass and towards the promised land: her *own* short mailbox on a quiet street, stuffed with the current month's *Town & Country* magazine, the seasonal *Ballard*

Home & Garden Designs catalogue, and a *Fidelity Investments* easy-to-read-market report, all attesting to the Good Life of a Mr. and Mrs. Tripp Sperling Whitley.

—⁓—

Tripp's sorry ass was comfortably nestled in the deep valley of the second-hand, stained, and oversized Barco-lounger that took up much of his studio apartment, and he was half listening to Gillian on his phone. The connection was also poor, something gone funky in some satellite somewhere over, or between, Gillian's apartment back East and Tripp's studio in the lively Country Club Plaza area of Kansas City.

"Wha...?"

"Tripp." She slipped into that slow rolling cadence which meant trouble, especially on a long-distance call. "What I said is, we're not moving *forward* as a couple because all you do is hang around with your *single* buddies." She paused. "Mostly divorced single buddies, acting like infants, always complaining about their ex-houses and ex-dogs and making up shit sitting around the bar at Gallihan's."

"Gallagher's."

This was Tripp's neighborhood hang-out, a pub with a selection list of beers as long as an Irish grudge and the best corned-beef-and-cabbage in the city. Word around the bar was that the census had tallied him as living there. Maybe most of his buddies, too, early thirty-somethings with mostly respectable jobs but wearing, as Gillian never failed to remind him, the various hues of domestic dysfunction, disaster, and defeat.

"Whatever, Tripp. It's been over two years now with this long-distance dating shit, and you are being pulled backwards." She paused. "That idiot Randy Lutz is the worst of all, you know. The last time we joined him for a beer at Gallihan's..."

"It's *Gallagher's*, Gillian. Gallagher's Irish Pub &..."

"...you're off somewhere, and I'm left sitting in a booth with this nitwit. He can't carry on a normal conversation even before three beers, so he takes a soggy napkin and starts drawing some kind of screwy graph with a sharpie like we're back in eleventh grade. I mean, who carries a sharpie around? Anyway, it's kind of melting on the soggy napkin as he writes it, so he just gives up and starts babbling on about something he called the *Lutz Equation,* claiming it's pretty much the most significant discovery since gravity, or maybe that dark matter in the universe, or maybe even that low-carb beer that actually tastes good. Crazy stuff, but you know Lutz. But he insists he invented it, and that it's going to change the world."

"Wha…*What?*" Tripp thought he heard something about his pal changing the world, and that dialed him into the call. Scared him, too. "Changing the world? Randy Lutz?"

"That's right. What he said. Anyway, he then looks at me funny and says '*You're textbook, Gillian.*' About that time, thank God, you came back. He shrugs, then drops it, and I still have no idea what he was talking about. But here's what I really think: this is all part of the larger problem, Tripp. I don't know how to fit in out there. I mean, I never even know if I'm in Kansas City, Kansas, or Kansas City, Missouri, or if they're even the same, much less having to deal with this kind of nonsense when I get near to your…"

"I live in Missouri…"

"Whatever. You need something else out there, something away from all this." Gillian paused. "*Them,* Randy. All of them, that whole clown circus." Tripp could hear her rustling something. "Look, I'll be out there in a couple weeks, plenty of time for you to set up a dinner with normal people, *married* people." She paused. "How about that nice guy down the hall in your law firm, Dan Pritchard? I think he graduated Penn a few years before I did. Played tennis too. Wife's in real estate."

"I think…"

"I met them when they hosted your firm party last year at their home, and I liked them. Maybe we do the full domestic. We offer to host, but they will suggest their home instead, your apartment likely known around town as a Superfund-site candidate on the short list. We agree, and offer to bring a salad and the wine. They cook up something that doesn't come in a pizza box, and we eat on a nice table set with real silverware and glasses, maybe even their good crystal. I look around, and to my great delight I do not see a single plastic cup stamped with something idiotic like *Runner-up, 2007 Intra-Pub Softball League...*"

"But we almost won it all, Gillian, if that..."

"...then after dinner we sit around a quiet living room, on Lillian August wingchairs clothed in a soft pastel chintz and not a beer-sticky Naugahyde in a corner booth at your Galli... *Gallagher's*. A dog nuzzles Dan's tassel loafers while we chat like normal people, and I am further delighted to hear an adult conversation that is not only sober but about something other than the line in Vegas on the first round of the NFL draft, or whether the smart money's on a classic '67 GTO over a Corvette, or how some sleazy bar is holding a Jello-wrestling contest—all the chicken wings you can eat for five bucks, the Jello a tangy strawberry—the whole thing bringing back a very bad memory of a small indiscretion on spring break in my—"

"*You Jello-wrestled?*" This conversation, Tripp thought, might still move in a more promising direction.

"That's not the point, Tripp. You need to grow up. All of you."

Tripp had hoped for a little more about that spring break *indiscretion*, but could see the dead end there. "All right, Gillian. Dinner with Mr. and Mrs. America." Tripp tried but failed to bottle-up the sigh, which by some tic in the orbit of the communications satellite amplified it.

"Come on, Tripp. You can handle this. Just *observe,* maybe think of yourself as Margaret Mead on some undiscovered atoll in the South Pacific."

—⁓—

"You're an idiot, Tripp."

Randy Lutz was buying the Monday night beers at Gallagher's and Tripp had just finished a replay of his phone call with Gillian the night before. He had gone heavy on the delicious scrap about Gillian's Jel-lo-wrestling *indiscretion,* and light on the proposed dinner adventure. *"Focus,* Tripp. You still think this dinner is all about you being, what did Gillian say, like Margaret Mead on some South Pacific atoll? The girl's twenty-five, man, and you've been dating, what, two years? Long-distance, too. How's that going for you two?" Randy looked over to the bar crowded with the long-distance-dating-wounded, and then pointed to the plastic Christmas tree at the end. "It's five weeks until Christmas, and this is important for you to remember." Randy paused. *"Very* important. And she's coming out here the weekend after next, right?"

Tripp nodded.

"Trouble, that's what you're in." Randy shook his head. *"She's in The Arc. It's textbook."*

The Arc?

Tripp expected the usual nonsense from his pal, but only after the third beer. This popped out with a sip left in the first. And it was the second time in less than twenty-four hours that the word *textbook* was linked to his friend. "Hold it right there, Randy. Gillian mentioned something about a textbook last night, and a graph you were trying to draw for her on a soggy napkin..."

"The Lutz Equation."

"The what?"

"The Lutz Equation. Been working on it for over a year." Randy paused to signal for a beer. "Ever since...well, you remember when Marnie took off with..." Randy sputtered, and let it drop.

Everyone around Gallagher's remembered that disaster, Randy moaning that he never saw it coming until one evening—just before going out to dinner, he always added, fancy reservations at Pier-pont's—the whole thing exploded. Gillian bought none of it, telling Tripp *anyone* could see it coming, that he should have looked for the cracks long before it was too late.

"Anyway," Randy picked it up, "the Equation's formal name is *The Randolph William Lutz, Jr., Linear Theory of Relationship Expectations.*

I was hoping to work out a few kinks before sharing it with you and the rest of the guys, but…"

Tripp shook his head. "Just what are we talking about here, Randy."

Randy pulled a black sharpie from the pocket of his coat.

Who carries a sharpie around?

"What we're talking about, my friend, is nothing less than a multi-dimensional, fully calibrated metric which can predict, *with near-certainty*, when the music and the laughs and the bullshit stops and someone calls the cards in any relationship, when the whole thing is about to crack apart." Randy looked like he was trying to find the right words, often a struggle. "And then, when the hammer comes down, the pieces just drift away like those chunks off the ice shelves at the north pole."

"Antarctica, Randy. The *south* pole."

"Whatever. The point is they just float away."

Randy then took a napkin, a crisp one this time from the corner of the booth, and began drawing a graph with his sharpie. On the left vertical axis he wrote *EXPECTATIONS* in large letters. Underneath, starting at the bottom, he wrote *LOW, MEDIUM, and HIGH* in smaller letters. He next drew the horizontal axis, labeling it *AGE*. He added numbers beginning on the left with 18, where the two axis lines meet, and continuing across the horizontal axis until stopping at 40. He then began peppering the graph with a series of dots, once again beginning at the left, at 18 on a point about halfway between *LOW* and *MEDIUM* on the vertical. As Randy dotted his way across the graph, they moved up and down, sometimes sharply.

"You paying attention here, Tripp?"

"Well, it's upside down, Randy…"

Randy ignored Tripp. "It's *all in here*, Tripp. Just you watch now." He then began to connect the dots with a line, a line which soon became a study in wavy grace, a geology-on-napkin of sharply rising twin peaks—the highest at Age 25, the second highest at Age 30—along with plummeting valleys and a small mostly flat plateau running slightly downhill from Age 37 to 40. "But I'm not finished, Tripp. This is just the basic stuff, pure metrics. What I am about to show you is what you most need to know, and know *now*."

Tripp was losing interest. Monday night was big-screen football at Gallagher's, and graphs of any kind brought back bad memories of when he once thought he might major in economics. "Come on, Randy, the game's about on."

Randy again ignored his pal, and began to draw a large, puffy cartoon cloud high above the graph line of peaks and valleys. In the cloud he wrote THE ARC OF EXPECTATIONS. Under it he then drew four smaller clouds. In the first, he wrote THANKSGIVING, in the second THE HOLIDAYS, in the third NEW YEAR'S EVE, and in the last VALENTINE'S DAY. None of the four small clouds hung lower on the Expectations scale than HIGH, although VALENTINE'S DAY seemed to have caught a little up-draft. Randy then drew a dashed line which raced straight over from the top of the High Expectation mark until it was right below THE HOLIDAYS cloud, and then dropped straight down through the highest peak on the graph until it landed precisely at Age 25.

"Randy…"

"Almost." Randy then enlarged and darkened the spot where the dashed lines met, adding GILLIAN HALL, tossed in an exclamation point, and handed his masterpiece to Tripp. "You now hold *The Lutz Equation*, my gift to you." It looked like this:

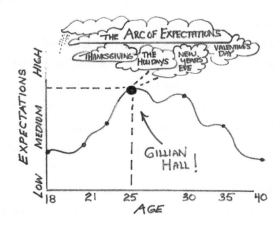

"You will observe, sir, that I have also added a small rain cloud in the upper left corner, warning that you are a fool if you do not understand that Gillian Hall is at the *single highest point* on The Arc of Expectations. She is, as I have now told you both, *textbook*: she's twenty-five, and you've been playing this thing out for almost two years." He waved towards the plastic tree. "And Christmas is just weeks away. You getting all this, Tripp?"

"Well, I guess …"

"No guessing around here, buddy. You better be Margaret Mead going to that dinner with a ring in your rucksack, Tripp Whitley. Gillian's not waiting around forever. It's *the Lutz Equation,* and it's, like, the law."

—◊◊◊—

The Pritchards greeted Tripp and Gillian at the door in full marital parade-rest dress.

Dan sported a blue blazer, open oxford shirt, grey slacks, and Johnson & Murphy tassel loafers as promised, with a dull shine that suggested a certain studied indifference. Sharon met the challenge with a simple sheath dress, dark blue and St. John's all the way, and matching pumps. All very East Coast, but not over the top. That seemed to please Gillian, although she and Tripp had dialed it back a notch, both of them in khaki slacks and sweaters.

Tripp brought along the salad and wine from Whole Foods, Gillian a thoughtful hostess gift of dark chocolates. The dinner itself was whipped up by Dan—a heaping plate of hand-cut pork medallions, sauteed and served with a diced Granny Smith apple sauce and roasted asparagus with a light bernaise—while Sharon bonded with Gillian in the living room, mostly about their backhands. After dinner, twin eight-year-old-year girls were trotted out, scrubbed to adorable. They smiled, said hello and goodnight in quick succession, then were gently dispatched to their bedroom. Gillian winked at Tripp when an overweight springer spaniel appeared from nowhere and began nuzzling Dan's tassels. The dog, however, quickly lost interest and headed to an oval knotted-rug by the fireplace, yawned, and fell asleep.

"How about a nightcap?" Dan moved over to a wet-bar tucked in a small study toward the back of the house. Tripp followed, and noticed for the first time that the Pritchards were adding a small addition to the back, and it had been hidden by a clear plastic sheet. The sheet was cracked and flapping at the bottom, a chill draft seeping in.

"Brandy?"

"Just a club soda, lime."

"Gillian?"

"She's fine, thanks." Tripp had been going easy on the booze, and mostly just observing during the dinner as Gillian had suggested. She had, however, prepared for him a few conversation starters should he wish to jump in, and one of them was home remodeling. He also knew enough about home improvement disasters from his ex-homeowning pals that a little yakking on a contractor would likely play well. "You know Dan, you may want to talk to your contractor about that flap."

"Yeah. It's been like that for a week." Dan shrugged. "Contractor's a real jerk. Should've been finished months ago. Don't know what he's doing."

Tripp nodded, although he not been near a contractor in his life.

Dan handed Tripp his drink, and nodded toward the living room. "We like her, Tripp."

Not for the first time that evening Tripp wondered when the "*marital we*" took over. Maybe at night, he thought, when couples are asleep, like the movie with the pod people.

—ᗰ—

On their drive back to his apartment after dinner, Tripp even suggested that they do dinner with the Pritchards again, maybe even on her next visit. He told Gillian he had actually enjoyed the evening, although he went easy on his concern about the pod people as well as the contractor and the hole in the back of the Pritchard's home. He also let stand, without further comment, what he thought was a rather tedious conversation about mortgage rates that had broken out just before Sharon's homemade coconut-cream pie dessert.

Gillian thought a re-play a terrific idea, and said she had enjoyed the evening too. "And," she added, "how about those pork medallions Dan cooked up?"

"Yeah, and how about my Whole Foods Salad-in-a Bag?"

"You're a jerk, Tripp."

—◊—

Gallagher's was quiet, a mid-March storm pounding the city outside. Tripp was settled into a corner booth, twirling the ice cubes in his drink, a second-shelf bourbon.

"You're late, Randy."

"Don't be a jerk, man. It's like an ice sheet out there." Randy settled in. "No one ought to be out on a night like this." He looked at his friend. "You okay? You don't look so good."

Tripp shrugged, then polished off his drink. It was clearly not his first. "Good to see you too, Randy. Been a while." Randy had been somewhere in Florida for weeks, wrapping up another business deal of uncertain virtue. No one ever quite knew what he did, although it seemed to have something to do with transportation logistics. "You remember how I told you I had a feeling something was just a little too, well, *perfect* when Gillian and I had that dinner over at the Pritchards, just before Christmas? Something *off,* that's what I felt."

"Well, you said you were going to be like Margaret Mead, *observing.* Checking things out. But I think you said you actually enjoyed yourself, although you did mention something about a contractor, and a hole in the house. Something else about pod people..."

"Yeah, you remember. Anyway, everything apparently blows up

over there in that perfect colonial on Windermere Lane just after you left for Tampa, around the second week of January. Dan starts coming in to my office every day telling me Sharon was fooling around with that contractor the whole time, why the job was taking so long. '*A stupid contractor*' he's yelling at me. '*She's begging me to forgive and forget*,' he's telling me. But no, he's '*done, **done!***' he tells me. One day he starts talking about '*other cracks in the ice*,' like he wants me to dig, but I don't. Anyway, he's talking about starting over, back East. '*Philadelphia*,' he says, reminding me he was Law Review at Penn, an uncle in a firm out there always asking him to join, cousins there for the girls, everything going to work out."

"Well, I've been there, you know."

"You were a *contractor*?"

"You're a jerk, Tripp. Just move it along."

"Anyway, next thing I know he's quit the firm, and actually headed back East."

"To Philadelphia?"

"Yeah. But it gets better."

Randy Lutz wasn't so sure about that.

"So yesterday I run into Sharon Pritchard, over at the Whole Foods. Yeah. I've started to like their salads. Anyway, she gives me this... *look*. Like to kill me, Randy." Tripp took a drink. "Then, right in front of an older couple picking out some endive lettuce, she's screaming at me '*Your little Gillian's been takin' up with Dan, you idiot.*' I don't know what to do, or think." Tripp paused. "I mean, Gillian mentioned a month or so ago that she had run into Dan. Some bar, just by chance."

"And..."

"So I call Gillian this afternoon, and do you have any idea what she told me. *Any—ANY—idea, Randy?*"

—⁜—

Randy Lutz had a *very good* idea, all right. He took some comfort in knowing that he had tried to warn his buddy of the forces at play, although he knew that Tripp had failed to pack anything into his rucksack on his Margaret Mead Christmas-time adventure at the Pritchards that looked anything like a ring, or even a promise. Just a Whole Foods Salad-in-a-Bag, as he remembered his buddy telling him.

The twice-divorced architect of the *Randolph William Lutz, Jr., Linear Theory of Relationship Expectations* also knew when a pal doesn't want an answer, and just needs a friend.

The Night Train

"It's coming, boy."

"The night train, Grampa?"

"Yep. *The Flyer*." Lucas Peteet paused, his voice deep and cloudy. He had been a railroad man, working mostly the freights out of Chattanooga on the Dixie Line. His massive arms told local folks that he was a locomotive fireman, his job to stoke the hungry coal-fired boiler on the Pacific 4-6-2's, the rugged, steam-belching monsters favored by the Southern railroads, including his Louisville, Nashville & West Ashley.

He turned to his grandson. "Hear it?"

The boy cupped his ear, as he always did, turning towards the darkness.

"Cain't hear nothin', Grampa."

The boy walked to the edge of the porch of the house they now shared, a tidy white wooden three-bedroom built on low brick supports. The house sagged ever so gently, like most of the houses close along the old railroad right-of-way, houses burdened by the hardscrabble rural life and settling unevenly into the soft red Georgia clay.

He leaned out. "Nothin' but them katydids and tree frogs." The boy paused. "And Miss Louise fussing at her dog again, out past the barn."

A light mist had started to fall—a young fog dancing among the live oaks and loblolly pines and the small patch of land they worked. Beans, mostly.

"It's coming, boy." The old man stared into the darkness. "It's coming."

—ɷ—

Lucas married a week after he hired on to the railroad just months before the Great War, the one to end all wars. She had just turned eighteen, a quiet girl from Slope's Corner everyone called Sunny for her straw-blond hair, cut close, and her bright sky-blue eyes. Her people upstate would say later that they had hoped more for her than what a railroad man, an *older* man, could offer.

But Lucas was honest and kind and hard-working, and the railroads were doing well. They quickly set out to build a life in the little white house, and it was a good one.

Just after her twenty-first birthday they welcomed a son. He was born in the back bedroom, arriving to the sounds of the night train racing its way south, heading to New Orleans. They named him Tommie. He was a happy baby who grew up—so quickly, they would say—on the hard scripture of the local Reformed Pentecostal Church, his mama's legendary biscuits and gravy, and the dusty red clay of the ballparks of South Georgia where his graceful play at shortstop—his rocket throws from deep infield to first were legendary—caught the eye of several scouts. The Senators signed Tommie a week after graduation, sending him to their Southern Association Double-A team in Chattanooga in June of 1941.

Lucas swapped crews so he could take his boy up there—*took him up there myself on the 10:48*, he liked to say.

—ɷ—

After the season ended Tommie married a local girl, Maribeth Tresley. It was a quiet home ceremony, just family and a few friends. As the local afternoon freight chugged its way past the little white house, the reception spilled gently on to the porch to hear its special chorus of bells and whistles—*just a little salute to the newlyweds*, that's what folks said. Tommie and Maribeth just smiled as they knew the engineer was Lucas's best friend.

—⟁—

Four months later, Tommie was drafted and sent to Louisiana for basic.

And on a moonless night in April of 1942, Tommie's troop train sped past his boyhood home. He looked, but couldn't see, three people standing on the porch: his mama and papa, each holding a small American flag and their tears back, and his bride, holding an overstuffed teddy bear that Tommie had won for her at the county fair a week after they were married, knocking down all the milk bottles with a single throw. They said they would agree on what to name it, someday, but never got around to it before Tommie left for the war.

No one knew then that Maribeth was pregnant, or that Tommie would never play ball again.

—⟁—

Late in the war, along a nameless stream in a forgotten village in France, Cpl. Tommie Peteet caught a round in his right shoulder, shattering bone and muscle. The bleeding was stopped just in time by a medic and—as Tommie wrote to Maribeth—by the Grace of God. He also said the docs did a good job of patching him up, although he had lost much of the motion in his throwing arm. He would be coming back to the States on a troop ship, docking in Brooklyn sometime mid-November. He would then work his way home, the last leg on the night train from Louisville. Lucas pulled a few strings to get assigned to *The Flyer* for a few months, just so he could bring his son home.

Four days out, the troop ship was sunk by a torpedo.

And a week after Thanksgiving of 1944, the War Department notified the family that Tommie was among the missing. Lucas quit the railroad a month later, and within a year the Dixie Line itself was abandoned.

—⚏—

The night was still, and the boy restless. He had been through this before, his grampa slipping a few steps sideways, talking about the night train again and walking out to the porch to stare into the darkness.

"Grampa," the boy said softly, "it's not coming tonight."

He was almost eight now, and he loved his grandfather. He also loved the father he had never seen, but it was hard—like trying to capture a firefly on a hot summer night. But all the boys during the war had grown up fast.

"Your papa's coming home, on the night train." The railroad man paused. "That's what he told us."

"I know, Grampa."

He took his grandfather's hand, and walked him slowly from the edge of the porch and over to the wooden rockers by the front door. "Sit with me Grampa, and tell me again how my papa won that teddy bear for my mama, and how the fresh-mowed grass in the old county ballparks smelled in the early spring, and how you stoked the train that took my papa up to Chattanooga before the war."

The boy paused. "And tell me about the night trains too, and how they brought the boys home."

Ronald Reagan in the Time of the Plague

It had been a quiet day when Ronald Reagan showed up at Rick Knapp's front door, quite unexpectedly.

As a well-worn sixty-something, Rick did not like surprises.

That it *was* Mr. Reagan was not, however, in doubt: tall, a wide grin and an enviable thickness of dark hair, particularly for a man his age; a loose-fitting blue chambray shirt; a pair of Levi jeans; scuffed cowboy boots. It wasn't quite the Florida country-club-casual vibe Rick was used to seeing around his not-quite-gated retirement community in Vero Beach, and Mr. Reagan was a little smaller than he remembered.

But he thought the Gipper still looked pretty good.

Rick could not place the woman who was with Mr. Reagan, at least not immediately: a pair of over-sized sunglasses shielded her eyes, and a stylish mask covered her nose and mouth, fitting uncomfortably behind her ears. It looked homemade, perhaps beginning its life as a bright floral design dancing around a lightweight summer blouse before things started going bad. Rick, who had lived alone for years, rarely wore his red bandana, and certainly not around his house. He didn't think it made a difference anyway, although he was quietly warming up to this "social distancing" thing, the widows backing off from their earnest, but tedious, invitations.

Rick Knapp, as he often told his long-time friend Will Pierce, was *one and done*, and Will understood.

Standing at the door and backlit by a retiring sun, the woman looked like she was headed out for a late afternoon glass of wine, perhaps a rich Tuscany Chianti—or even two—on the patio of Trattoria Dario on Ocean Drive. Maybe in her late thirties, she was wearing lime-green pants dotted with what looked like small martini-glasses, a simple white blouse, a light cotton sweater, and a pair of Ferragamo flats. Her blonde hair was pulled back in a ponytail, stylish in a brisk and understated professional way. She slid her sunglasses upward to rest atop her head. Her eyes—*those eyes*—were alive with something special, searching, deep, and... familiar.

He had known eyes like that only once.

"Hello, Rick."

The voice—*yes, that voice*—

"I've missed you."

It was softer than he remembered it when in the late fall of 1984 they'd met in Washington, and she introduced him to Mr. Reagan.

But that was a long time ago, when facts were simply facts and people weren't dying from a friend's touch, a child's hug, or a lover's embrace.

"Ellie..."

—◊—

On the morning Rick Knapp met Ellie Heywood, he was enjoying an oversized lox and bagel sandwich, with a side of sweet slaw and a second high-test Coke, in the back of Tips' Place, a feisty café two blocks from DuPont Circle owned by his friend Will Pierce.

Rick and Will had been best friends growing up in Crook's Bend, Georgia, where their families enjoyed deep roots in the dusty soil and fabric of Talbot County and cornered a nice slice of the market for good works: their mothers volunteered at the Church Mouse Thrift Store, operated in town with a quiet dignity by the Good Shepherd Baptist Church, and their fathers ushered at the early Sunday service. After graduating from a small day-academy the boys headed off to Southern together, Rick on a partial Rotary scholarship and Will as a walk-on tight end for the Eagles.

It took a year for Rick to find his footing as a major in political science with a minor in economics, and a little longer for Will, a sports management major with a minor in the ladies of Kappa Kappa Gamma. Rick earned his degree in 1980, and quickly landed a job in Washington as a staff aide to a four-term Democratic congressman from Kentucky. Will graduated two years later, and less quickly signed as a free agent with Washington.

Rick's eager charm of the pudgy Southern sort played well, along with a quiet confidence tucked behind his ready grin. He always remembered to keep the middle button of his three dark blue suits fastened—something a pal over at the State Department swore was the secret to career success, and it also made him look thinner. He also practiced a personal politics of the more liquid sort, a kind of *due process liberalism*. This was a very useful currency in Washington, its very formlessness promising something for everybody. That seemed to be the trick in a city like Washington.

His friend Will learned a few things too—mostly that a free-agent tight end who bounced, with surprising regularity, long downfield passes off the tips of his fingers gets slapped with a nickname quickly, and rarely of the noble sort.

His was *Tips*.

Almost as quickly he earned his release from the team, stumbling a bit until he bought into a failing bar with a couple of former teammates. Part of the deal was Will's nickname coming along for the ride, and the job of managing the place. Re-opened as Tips' Place, with a new up-market feel and a little boost from Rick around the Hill, young congressional staffers soon flocked to the place for the best weekend brunch in town. It also didn't hurt that most thought the place had some connection to the Speaker of the House, and, like Rick's liquid politics, this all became a bit of useful local mythology, good for business.

Will Pierce let it ride, just shrugging when some bright young congressional staffer complained that no one had actually ever *seen* the Speaker there, or gently suggested that someone should fix the apostrophe.

Yes, Rick had been enjoying his Saturday morning, the city's big Inauguration Bash still almost two months away, the tourists few. He had tuned out the annoying political chatter around the tables, mostly talk of the Reagan landslide, and was once again happily eating the fresh and notably large Tips' Place bagels after ending a once-promising relationship with a tall, annoyingly trim and carb-phobic staffer at the Congressional Budget Office.

—⚏—

And on that pleasant Saturday in the fall of 1984 Ellie Heywood did not so much *walk* into Rick's life, as *stumble* in.

All five-foot-five of her holding on to Ronald Reagan, tightly.

Or more precisely, holding on to an almost life-sized cardboard cut-out of the president, the kind which had popped up during the fall campaign in political curio shops all over town, just begging to be bought by tourists from Omaha and Young Republican political science majors from just about anywhere.

And if not many of the regulars in Tips' Place were quite ready for this, Rick was enjoying the sight.

"I guess I need a table for two," Rick heard her say to Will Pierce, who was working the place this morning.

"Guess so." Will looked amused. "Unless you can fold Mr. Reagan in half and stick him under the table."

Ellie smiled. "The president? Please."

Will liked her. "How about that table in the back, next to the guy sitting alone with his *Post*?" Will nodded toward Rick's table in the rear, and Rick smiled.

She looked, then shrugged. "Sure," she said, then hesitated. "You know the guy?"

"Yeah, a good guy. Works on the Hill."

"He a Republican?"

Will laughed. "Calls himself a *due process liberal*."

"Sounds like a bunch of Democratic nonsense." But she said it with a light tone. "I just hope he doesn't mind if I bring my friend along."

She threaded her way to the back, holding the president carefully at the waist, and high. This worked well, at least for the sitting patrons: not a one got beaned, although the president took a glancing blow to his handsome cardboard head of hair on a low-hanging light, with just a tiny nick. She sat down at the table next to Rick's, and propped Mr. Reagan up against the wall.

"Hi. I'm Ellie Heywood, and this is your president."

"And I'm Rick Knapp, and I know that."

"For another four years, too."

"I know that too."

It was, as these things go, a curious introduction, but one that they would happily enjoy telling their many friends for years. And if Rick missed that little jab, he was already lost in Ellie Heywood's eyes— large, dark pools which, many years later, he would think were like those of Anne Hathaway, only better.

—⁂—

Ellie was not from Omaha, but an upstate South Carolina girl in her senior year at Maryland. She was, however, a political science major and a Young Republican, with an application to the Fletcher School of Law and Diplomacy in the works. She had come to town for the day with three girlfriends to buy the cardboard president for a campus YR event, planning to meet them for a beer at The Tombs in Georgetown later that day before driving back to College Park.

Rick learned these basics before her order of a cheese croissant and sweet iced tea arrived, and by the time they decided to split an extra-large slice of apple crumb cake they had fallen into an easy, laugh-rich banter of things important and silly and funny and sad—the timeless stuff of two young people already sensing something special. Mr. Reagan had been a most accommodating third wheel, generous in both his silence and growing—if imagined—approval.

Will could see it too, and when eight months later he hosted their engagement party at Tips' Place he served everybody huge slices of a cinnamon-rich, walnut-stuffed apple crumb cake. Mr. Reagan was there, of course, once again propped up against a back wall. Ellie told Rick the Gipper approved, but wasn't buying any of that liquid political currency nonsense.

—⚏—

Theirs was a good marriage, pupping a son in their second year and building together a quiet life in the foothills near Leesburg, Virginia. They both taught at Foxcroft, a small private school nearby, and twice a month they would drive over to the Red Fox Inn for their Sunday brunch of smoked duck hash, and once a month into Washington to Tips' Place, always splitting an apple crumb cake. They dared not take their son to the charming quiet of the Inn, but they would always take him to see "Uncle Will," who never tired of telling young Ronnie Knapp all about how he was named.

They would laugh about lives writ smaller than they once would have imagined: she far removed from a foreign service career; Rick from a seat in Congress; and Will from professional football. But Ellie was quick to add that she was quite content to send others to the distant lands, her work as faculty coordinator for the school's Foreign Exchange Program engaging and fun. Rick would nod, perhaps less inclined to jump in with tales of his daring service to the people of his community on the local Zoning Commission. Will Pierce would look around at his many friends and an always packed house, and smile too.

The years never etched away their laughter. It was easy and generous, and sometimes shared with just a knowing look. Yes, that's what people would always say, how joyous was their laughter.

Until, one wintry night early in 1997 on a back road six miles out-side Middleburg, the laughter was stilled. The night was dark, the ice black, the couple returning home from a faculty event of no real im-portance. Rick, behind the wheel, never saw it coming. He tried to smooth the spin but over-corrected, sending their Subaru into a ditch. Both were banged up, their bruises seeming minor, with the EMTs quick to the scene. He would later tell Will that Ellie looked okay, her Anne Hathaway eyes bright, her voice calm and mildly scolding.

"You almost had it..."

—✳︎—

Under the chill pink of a winter late-afternoon sky, Ellie Heywood Knapp was buried behind the historic Church of Our Saviour, along the James Monroe Highway in Oatlands, Virginia. She was six days short of her thirty-fifth birthday.

Rick and Ronnie Knapp stood together under an overcast sky, moved to quiet tears as the many friends of Ellie Knapp joined in the singing of Hymn 473, *Lift High the Cross*. Rick had asked that her cas-ket be lowered into the hard-frozen soil with the mourners present so that those who wished could dust her casket with a sprinkle of dirt. Many did, knowing that the dirt had come a long way, from a past stu-dent's first foreign service: she had brought it with her in a silver flask from her posting in Sao Paulo. And as the last shaft of light caught the polished brass handle of her casket, Rick Knapp knew then that he would, someday, be fine.

It would just take a while.

—✳︎—

Rick continued to teach, a good man living a quiet life, and he never remarried. Over the years he found joy in his son, meaning in the success of his students at Foxcroft, and comfort in his Faith. On

Sundays he would sit in the same aged pew and listen to the gentle ser-
mons of the Rev. T. James Bay, the lessons of Testaments both Old and
New, and the searching words of the Episcopal Hymnal, *Eternal Father* especially. He always looked forward to the quiet gathering of the
parishioners in the simple white clapboard parish house afterwards,
the biscuits freshly baked by the pastor's gracious wife, the ham sliced
just right, the lemonade in the summer tangy and cold, the coffee in
the winter hot and strong. He would linger long after the others were
gone—the Reverend and his wife understood—before walking up the
small hill to the cemetery to listen to the soft whispers of the pines in
the winter, and the rustle of the oaks and maples in the summer.

In June of 2017 Rick took an early retirement, gifting his modest
collection of books to the school. He sold his small home quickly and
well, and nudged South—first to Myrtle Beach, which he did not like,
then on to Vero Beach, which he did.

He was planning a cruise—his second, a quick five-day deal out of
Lauderdale, just long enough to tag Cozumel and return—when Ce-
lebrity pulled the plug on all their sailings after the virus hit. Rick had
convinced Will to book it too, and the two old friends were looking
forward to a floating visit, including those fancy drinks with the paper
umbrellas which were never on the menu at Tips' Place.

But they decided, two older men now living alone and things being what they were, to do a little better in keeping up. They agreed on
a weekly call, rotating who called whom.

It was Rick's week when Will got the call from Ronnie Knapp, early
on a Tuesday evening.

"You heard from my dad, Will?" The *uncle* had disappeared when
Ronnie entered the Fletcher School of Law and Diplomacy.

"No, just waiting for our weekly call, matter of fact. His turn." Will
paused. "Yeah, a day late, he is."

"Maybe nothing, Will. But I got a funny feeling from the message
he left on my machine this afternoon. Dad sounded…" Ronnie paused.
"Dad didn't sound right. Said he was looking forward to a nice glass

of wine, maybe two, with Mom, over to that place on Ocean Drive, something about Reagan joining them too. You know, I still have that cardboard cut-out, stored away. Thought maybe he was just…"

—⁊⊓—

The EMTs measured Rick Knapp's temperature at 104.7 when they found him, his shorts and shirt soaked, his bedsheets twisted around his feet. He was incoherent, his breathing labored and shallow, his lungs already turning into a wooden mass.

But Rick Knapp had a glass of wine in mind, a rich Tuscany Chianti—or maybe two—to enjoy with his wife. *I miss you,* she'd said, and he didn't want to keep her waiting.

Or Mr. Reagan either.

Customer Service

"Now you be nice to those people at the bank today, Richard. You know you don't play so well with people anymore."

Richard Frobush, "Ferbie" to his oldest friends and just a few steps into retirement, *did* know this. But he could count on his wife's gentle reminder, regularly served-up with a sympathetic nod when he was about to re-enter—even for a moment—the world of the *actual-working*. It landed with a heavier marital thud, however, when she knew he was about to talk to someone at their bank, which had once been a quiet small-town institution known as Howerton State Bank & Trust, of Red Cedar, Iowa.

That bank, he would then remind his wife, had run along just fine under three generations of Howertons—a bank, he would add, with the sober feel of dark blue suits and ties, starched white shirts and polished mahogany desks, ornate brass teller cages and a slightly worn marble floor. Everything about it—particularly an enormous Herring-Hall-Marvin Co. vault dominating the back wall—told him that they were important, that their accounts were valued and their money safe. But most of all, that they were actually in a *bank*.

No, nothing like the fool Trans-Global Bank that gobbled it up three years ago, the whole place now looking like nothing more than a peppy Starbucks, serving up latte and bagels and donuts—the kind with the powdered sugar topping which can be blown away with nothing more than a child's sneeze. All the real banking seemed to be conducted in little conversation pits, with kids dressed in matching light blue polo shirts, Trans-Global—the name sounding more like a charter airline fly-ing questionable cargo on forty-year-old 727's out of Colombia than a bank—stitched across the left pocket. Even more alarming, the old vault was seemingly demoted in the re-model, now languishing somewhere be-hind four over-sized screens turned to CNBC, CNN, MSNBC and the BBC, and a built-in juice bar.

It now pained Richard Frobush to visit the bank. He was a man of limited interest in most things changed, unless he had no other option. But this morning he did: he would just call the bank's toll-free VIP Customer Service number to change his address, and hope the call lands somewhere in the United States.

Don't even have to change my shirt, he thought, as he marveled at the blotchy stain freshly etched into his favorite shirt, an oversized, butter-soft cotton oldie in a quiet plaid, its cuffs trailing a small army of threads.

—◊—

"Hello, and welcome to Trans-Global Bank's automated, twenty-four-seven toll-free VIP Customer Service Line. We see that you are calling from a number in your profile. Thank you. We do, however, apologize that we are experiencing unusual delays—"

What, whipping up a new batch of powdered donuts for the branch-es? Richard rarely got into trouble talking smack with the automated voices, and this he liked to do.

"—and your wait time will be approximately forty-seven minutes."

You kidding me? I can fly from here to Dubuque in less time, not that I want to this morning.

"Please press the '1' key if you wish to hold for the next available associate. If that is inconvenient—"

Just a bit it is, but thanks for asking. What else do I have to do? I mean, it's only that I'm pushing seventy, and my personal expiration date could be waiting at the end of that very same forty-seven minutes. I mean, I felt a couple funny thumps in my chest just last week. But why wouldn't I welcome this way to spend, possibly, the last precious moments of my near-expiration?

"—simply hang up, and try again later. You may be interested to know that waiting times are shortest after 1:30 in the morning—"

Only mildly interested, really. But thank you. It's just that I am pretty much asleep then, unless the gout kicks in. And you never want to talk to me then.

"—or you may wish to access our on-line banking app on your smart device."

I wish for many things, Global. May I call you Global? Good. But not this. And I hate my smart phone. Can't even find it today. Haven't for a couple days. Loved my flip phone though, all I ever needed. Still carry that beauty around, when I can remember where I put it, just to let folks see that I have crossed the techno divide, even if not very far. That change-over to Windows 10 nearly did me in last year, waiting to the very end, Windows 7 a good pal that I hated to see go. So I'll just put my phone on speaker, press that "1" key, close my eyes for a few moments, and drift off to your fine music—hey, maybe you folks can stitch a little Simon & Garfunkel into the playlist—and hope I wake up…

—⚘—

"Hello, and thank you for your patience. Please know that this conversation may be recorded for quality control and training purposes."

May be? You and I both know nothing's more fun at the end of some tedious training session in a cramped conference room at the local Holiday Inn Express in, say, Council Bluffs on a frigid February afternoon, than making fun of some befuddled old-timer unhappy with the techno-mysteries of the modern banking world.

"Now, if you are a current checking or savings account-holder, please press the '1' key."

That's the ticket. Door number one again. Grab it quick.

Richard pressed it, smartly avoiding any of the other exciting options on the automated customer service line which, untamed, he knew could lead him into some dark and nightmarish journey, like Martin Sheen going deep up-river in *Apocalypse Now*.

"Thank you. Please say or enter your account number, followed by the last four digits of your Social Security number."

Got 'em both here. Not my first rodeo, Global. I'm going with punch-the-numbers, checking account first.

Richard's fingers pecked across the phone keys.

"I'm sorry, but the account number does not match our records. Please try again."

Richard reached for his glasses—his Walmart cheaters, which his wife buys for him in twelve-packs—and put them on. *Much Better. Fuzzed out the 3 to an 8, Global. Sorry, but that shit happens all the time. No one ever tells you about this, you know, when you're young. Maybe someone should change one of those numbers, maybe add a little tail squiggle to the 8. Yeah, that's the play.*

"Thank you. Please enter the last four digits of your social security number."

Easy.

"Thank you, Mr. Richard Frobush, for banking with us for over forty-nine years."

Well, sure, if you include my happy forty-six years with Howerton State Bank and Trust, before you ate them. But you're welcome anyway. The merger was just business, I know. But I'm not so sure you should really take credit for those good years.

"What can we do for you today? Just pick a short phrase which best describes what you would like to do, like 'I want to open a Best-in-the-Business Trans-Global Titanium credit card.' Double cash-back points for your first year."

I'm fixed up pretty good there, Global. "I just need to change my address."

"*Just* change your address? How about opening that Best-in-the-Business Trans-Global Titanium credit card while we're at it?"

"No, just a change of address."

"Well, okay then. I am connecting you now to a Personal VIP Customer Relations Specialist."

—m—

"Good morning Mr. Froburn."

"Mr. Frobush."

"Sorry, Mr. Frobush, of course. My name is Charlotte—"

Sure it is. Your call center name, your professional name. Like the almost-stripper I knew when I was at Iowa State, a tall redhead just off the farm who swore she was named Cinnamon at birth, preferred to be called an "interpretative dance artist," and adopted the stage name "judi" with a heart over the 'i' and a lower case "j". Go figure. Anyway, she put herself through vet school on the tips she made dancing interpretatively and-not-quite-naked on Friday nights at the Dusty Barn Gentlemen's Club, and working three other nights a week at the county animal clinic. But it's your career here, Charlotte, and you just do what you need to do. But at least it sounds like you're not in India.

"Are you there, Mr. Frobush?"

"Sorry, I just drifted away for a minute." *Yeah, to a happier place. Enjoy every moment, Charlotte. It all goes by so fast.*

"Well, welcome back. Now, how can I help you today? Maybe go ahead and open up our Best-in-the-Business Trans-Global Titanium—"

"No. I thought I just told the computer I didn't want—"

"Well, we all know computers, right?"

"Right." He chuckled. *Sense of humor. Maybe we'll get through this without any real trouble today.* "Tell me about it, Charlotte. But all I want is to change my address."

"Alrighty then. Change of address. I just need to ask you a few security questions." She paused. "Ready?"

"You bet. I could use a little mental workout after this forty... forty nine minute pre-game." *Just a little smack-down, nothing my wife—*

"Yes, we've been experiencing unusual call volume."

"That's what I hear. The questions?"

"Certainly. What was the name of your first school?"

"First *real* school, like first grade? Or pre-school?" Richard Frobush, his wife also reminded him, overthinks things. It usually did not help matters.

"Sorry Mr. Frobush, no hints."

"I'll go with *real* schools for ten: Millard Fillmore Elementary."

"Ah, how about the name of your first dog."

"My first dog, or the first dog in my family? *Your* can be a tricky possessive, you know."

"No hints, like I just said, Mr. Frobush."

Richard remembered three family dogs, but not which one could really be tagged as *his*—which basically meant cleaning up puppy shit. He remembers he did that for two, his younger sister coming along in time to do the honors for the third. *And how the hell would they know that anyway? It's all a fake test, just to see if I fold.*

"Chester. A springer spaniel, blind in one eye." *Nice detail, confident. That's really what they're looking for.* "The idiot dog used to chow down on my father's Sunday-best lace-ups, without gastric distress. But he'd ralph his puppy chow, and drink out of the toilet. Also had a habit of humping any leg around—" *Dial it back, Buster Brown. This is the New Sensitivity.*

Charlotte sighed. "Maybe a little more than I need to know, sir. And we're not quite getting to the optimum... well, I need to ask a few more questions, multiple choice."

Damn, I knew I should have gone with the collie, the fat one named Lucy. And what the hell is this, an application for the National Security Agency?

"Multiple choice? I'm just trying to change my address here, Charlotte."

"Just procedure, sir. Won't take much longer. Account security is our most important responsibility."

Yeah, and sending my account statement to the right address ranks right up there too. And don't talk to me about going all-in online.

"Sir, you can avoid all this by switching over to our Best-in-the-Business VIP Online Banking."

Sure I can. But it's not gonna happen.

"Well, I'm now pushing an hour into this, Charlotte, what with the delay caused by unusual call volume. And my third dog—or maybe it was an "our" dog, a yappy terrier named Eli, a canine miracle now 423 years old in human years with a cranky old man's attitude like mine—just ate my computer. So it's a no-go on the online option. And quite frankly I am getting a little tired of all this." He paused. "What if I tell you I have a diagnosed case of acute bilateral anticipatory test anxiety syndrome?"

"Acute bi... *what?*"

"The fear of taking tests. Both sides of the brain, too. Untreatable, even over at Mayo. Haven't passed a test, any test, in years, and the last time I tried to take my driving license renewal check-ride I woke up in the hospital two days later, the left half of my body covered in a painful rash." *Now we're having fun.* "But only the *left* side. They told me that was very unusual for someone with *bilateral* acute—"

"Well, sir, let me see what we can do. Please hold."

—⚏—

"Mr. Frobush, I'm back. Thanks for your patience, and it looks like I can transfer you to another Customer Services Specialist who handles, uh... stuff. But I must tell you, due to—"

"Unusual call volume. Right. Let's just the two of us press on, Charlotte."

She thought I was serious.

"Fine. So which of the following towns have you lived in: Des Moines, Buffalo, Toledo, Bellows Corner? You may also choose 'None of the above.' "

"None of the above." *And where the hell is Bellows Corner anyway?*

"Which of the following cars have you ever owned: a Pontiac GTO, a Land Rover, a Jeep Wrangler, a Nissan Rogue?"

"A Jeep Wrangler. Maroon, tan seats. Low mileage, Charlotte. But who cares? I just want to change my fu—*you don't play well with people, Richard*—address. And how do you know all this stuff about me anyway?"

"That's proprietary, sir."

"You pick any of this crap up from that breach over at Equifax, personal stuff spilling out all over the place, maybe lying around bank floors all over the country ripe for the picking?"

"I can't answer that, sir. Now, have you ever lived at an address with the following zip codes: 29957, 35561, 20031, 79032?"

"You're kidding me." Richard paused. "I'm done with Twenty Questions. Get me a supervisor."

—m—

"Good morning, Mr. Frobush, My name is Jennifer, and I am the Escalation Manager"

The what? Richard thought.

"The what?" Richard asked.

"The Escalation Manager."

"The *Escalation* Manager." Richard let that slide off his tongue, slowly, just to take it all in. "How wonderful. I just wanted a *supervisor*, you know, to help me change my address." He paused. "I mean, I get that things *escalate*, like, say, tensions along the West Bank, or over there in Ukraine, or even around my Thanksgiving dinner table when that fool Uncle Jerry has that fourth shot of Wild Turkey. But *this?*"

Well, maybe that thing about Chester humping… "Like I said, I just want to change my address."

"Well, our VIP Customer Relations Specialist felt a little tension this morning, and our procedures—"

"Well, your procedures suck. I just want to change my—*Richard, play nice*—bloody address."

"Sir, that's *exactly* the kind of attitude we at Trans-Global call escalation—"

"I'm sure it is."

"—and, as Escalation Manager, I believe our Regional Escalation Manager may be better able to assist you at this point in our customer service. However, due to unusual—"

"Just get the fool Regional Escalation Manager on the line. *Now.*"

—⁂—

"Hello, Mr. Frobush. My name is Chandler, the Senior Trans-Global Regional Escalation Manager."

The **SENIOR** *Regional Escalation Manager? Ouch. Maybe I need a lawyer.*

"I understand you have experienced some disappointment with our identity-security procedures this morning."

Some disappointment? I mean—wait, that voice.

"Hey, Chandler, what's your last name?"

"Sir, we are not—"

You wouldn't be a Chandler *Mason Howerton,* would you? From Red Cedar, Iowa?

"I—"

"Dated my sister, Linda Susan? The old man popped you one when you brought her home from a date late one night."

"***Ferbie?*** *Ferbie* Frobush?"

Of the many daily humiliations on the playground of the Millard Filmore Elementary School—where the Darwinian struggles of the Serengeti look tame in comparison—an unwanted nickname, suddenly materializing out of nowhere, was among the cruelest.

"No one's called me that in a long time, Chandler. But, yes, it's me."

"Well, how about this."

"Yeah. How about it. But I gotta ask you, Chandler, what the hell's going on over there at Global? Nothing like when you Howertons owned the bank. And you? Weren't you, like, already an Assistant Vice Chairman of the Howerton Bank board when we went off to Iowa State? And now…?"

That came out a little hard. I liked the guy.

"Part of the deal, I guess. Just business. Soft landing and all that. Tucked out of the way, counting down to retirement. Damned Senior Regional Escalation Manager, can you beat it?" Chandler Howerton paused. "Anyway, so here *you* are, at the doorstep of the Senior Regional Escalation Manager, the cosmic machinery of the universe at its ironic best."

"This is not an existential moment, Chandler. I just want to change my address, but those questions are—"

"I know. Crazy. But no one listens to me. Let me look at what they've sent over." Chandler laughed. "I'm not going to put you on hold. This will take less than a minute."

—⁂—

The Senior Regional Escalation Manager was good to his word, back in a minute. "Even *I* knew that your first dog was Lucy, Ferbie. Everybody in town did, your sisters always complaining that Lucy's puppy shit was really the only shit you ever cleaned up."

"I *knew* I should have gone with Lucy, but—"

"You blew the computer profile, those zip codes a mess. Then you got a little, uh, suggestive, sending you off to Escalation. Happens a lot these days, but mostly to old guys like us. Look, I can override, get you back on track, kind of like that softy assistant dean in Ames cut us a break our junior year after that little problem after the Purdue game. No big deal, you remember. Talked our way right out of it. Same deal here. You need just one more correct answer—one that I can be absolutely sure about and then I can personally nudge you over the security threshold." Chandler laughed. "And nice try on that *acute bilateral whatever* bit. That's a new one." He paused. "I always had fun around you, Ferbie. Wish we had kept up after college."

"Me too." Richard laughed. "Look, I thought that bilateral testing bit could be a little fun, like a *de*-escalating moment. But listen, Chandler: can you really promise we end this torture with just one more question?"

"Just one, but two parts."

"Then you change my address?"

"You got it."

"I'll take the deal, Chandler. Shoot."

"Excellent call, Ferbie. The Dusty Barn had a tall redhead stripper—"

"Interpretative dance artist, Chandler—"

"—who headlined on Friday nights. Brilliant student at State, studying to be a vet. I can't remember if you ever actually dated her, but no matter. We all knew she had a given name, and another she danced under." Chandler laughed. "We encourage our folks on the VIP Customer Service Line to cook up a working name too."

Knew it.

"Always wondered what happened to her." Chandler seemed to take his own quick detour, then dialed back in. "Well, here's the deal: can you tell me her given name, and her, uh, professional name?"

—⚉—

"How'd it go with the address change, Richard?"

"Piece of cake, dear."

He smiled at his wife, knowing that the short answers never played well, the add-ons the better choice. She called them pathways to real conversations, healthy for the marriage at the end of the day. "And how was your day?"

"Could have been better, actually." She shook her hair, thick and rust-red. "A lot better. We're seeing a new strain of a nasty equine flu all over the county. Lost two horses today over at the Hassett place, three more just hanging on at the Buttontop Stables." She paused. "I could use a drink." She smiled. "And maybe a good story too. A reminiscence, maybe, about the old days…"

The Burden

In the first days after the storm he had trouble remembering things clearly, or even at all. His brain—suffering from what someone later told him was a kind of traumatic amnesia—simply couldn't cope with *now*. It went to a better time, and a better place. Actually, two better places: the towns of his childhood, reminders of a time long ago when all things seemed possible and fair, where *forever* had no horizon, and the killer storms lost their deadly appetite far from home.

But Parker Thompson understood that *possible* is largely a dividend of place and circumstance, *fair* can hinge on nothing more than a conceit born of chance, and *forever* is the stuff of dreams.

And he now knows that even a Category 2, at a Carolina high tide in the middle of the night, is a real brute.

—⁓—

He hadn't been back to either of his early homes in years, and likely wouldn't have gone except for the storm, a most unwanted visitor to his cottage along a coastal tidal marsh. An early October nightmare, it rudely bounced along the southeastern coast, a drunken sailor of a storm which slapped headlong into the home he and his wife had bought two months before retiring, over a decade earlier. Their years along the marsh had been good, transplants coming to love the quiet rhythms and sounds and sights of the Lowcountry: the crackling of the oyster beds at low tide, the rudderless drift of a weathered board unloosed from a neighbor's crabbing dock, the tangy bite of the mist over the marsh. The tidal waters, they had been told, were not only good for the soul, but their bodies as well. Indeed, their retirement had been unmarred by anything but the minor annoyances of age—until a clot took her away ten months earlier.

The clot had been lurking deep and silent within her, as deadly as those tics in the gentle breezes off the coast of Africa that roll west, and turn ugly.

—⁂—

Sometime after midnight the storm felled the two live oaks which had stood guard by the cottage, their gnarly branches, draping gracefully over the screened porch for over a century, dressed in clumps of Spanish moss. His wife often said the canopy made her feel safe, that it reminded her of the *church and steeple* her interlocked fingers had formed when as a child she had hidden in her family's storm shelter as dark clouds roiled in over her native Kansas horizon.

Tethered more loosely to his faith—his wife often teased him that he was a mere *Horticultural Christian,* gracing the Church of the Good Shepherd along the May River only when the flowers were plenty and center stage—Parker had clutched only a cell phone, a flashlight, and a tin box with his insurance papers when the trees finally smashed through his porch.

He had been a fool to ride it out.

At the peak of the storm, sometime around four-thirty in the morning, the French doors—the old kind which opened inward and were not to code—blew open. The rain drilled horizontally into the living room for hours, sparing few of the marital treasures his wife had so carefully arranged in the white bookcases which lined the wall—their son's Michigan State college mug, their daughter's wedding picture, a smoky-orange juggling pin they bought at a flea-market just outside

Williamsburg with its curious faded sticker reading *Birkenbach Sporting Goods, It Pays to Play, Columbus, Ohio.*

—ɯ—

He left his wounded cottage a week later, one of the lucky ones able to find a contractor to begin repairs. The death of his wife—and now the storm—had set him adrift, an old man waiting for his compass to settle down, unsure of how or even where to fill the next weeks, or months, or even years. He thought of driving south to visit his daughter in Sarasota and his son in Tampa, and both would have welcomed him. But something was pulling him backwards.

Home, he figured, was where old men go when lost.

And Parker Thompson had two to choose from.

One, a sleepy town south of Vicksburg, sits along a wide bend in the mighty Mississippi. This was where he was born, where he spent his earliest years and many summers, and where his parents now rest in the family plot in the cemetery along the High Bluff Road. Next to the wooden bandstand at the edge of town, high above the river, five flags have flown over the town in its colorful, if now faded, history.

The other, an even sleepier village in Vermont, sits along a forgotten branch of the Winooski River. It claimed him for his middle youth, until he went off to Colby College when he was nineteen. The village is tethered to something called a township—a strange Yankee jurisdictional quirk which no one really understands, each circling the other like a binary star system. It has seen only two flags fly over the town square, although Parker remembers when his pal Stoop Morgan ran-up the flag of Moldova on a dare.

Vermont, with that one curious exception, was tamer than the more exotic trespasses of his time in Mississippi. His Northern adventures were harnessed with friends named Rob and Scott and Bud, and measured in a crisp Yankee way; his frolics with cousins and kin Down South introduced a cast of Andy Joes and Beaus and Bunnys, with adventures born of the thicker stuff of tribal blood. Of the two towns, Parker Thompson would only say he loved them both, their pulls strong in nearly equal parts, and he would be right.

But he had rattled some cages when he decided to bury his wife in Beaufort rather than the family plot, and those wounds, in the Southern way, had not yet healed. Besides, October was always the crisp and colorful gift to the people of Vermont, and he had not been back in many, many years.

So that's where he headed, hoping both he and his six-year-old Volvo were up to the long drive.

—⁊⁊—

It was just where Parker Thompson had left it, the village of Miller's Crossing, Vermont.

As he neared town, and just past the old creamery, he noticed the first sure sign that he was home—*Lookout Rock*. Rising almost vertically and nestled between two ridges of the Green Mountains, it loomed over the edge of town, conclusively marking its eastern boundary. The sheer face of the out-cropping, catching the afternoon sun, was nearly as dramatic as he remembered.

He pulled off the road near an iron historical marker, the kind that pop up all over New England with chipped black letters against a white background. Someone had filled in all the "o's" with black paint, which was more annoying than funny.

Maybe Stoop Morgan's grandson, he thought. *Kids...*

Parker had rarely taken the time to read any of those markers as a boy, but he had the time now along with a new curiosity. The raised letters, even with the annoying solid "o's," told him that Lookout Rock, three miles from where he was standing, rose exactly 278 feet from its base. This was something of a disappointment, even now, since he— and kids for generations, he assumed—had it looming some *800* feet, and even capping out at a healthy thousand for those inclined to push the more dramatic. The vertical scar, the marker informed, was left behind from some mid-nineteenth century trap-rock quarry operation, now defunct.

He also learned that during the Revolutionary War the Green Mountain Boys set up a signal station atop the Rock to observe the movement of British troops along the invasion route between Canada and the colonies, something he vaguely remembered once learning.

If the history of the Rock was legitimately storied, the real magic of the place—at least for Parker Thompson—was an open-sided building, a lookout about the size of a two-car garage which sat at the top of the Rock in a small clearing. And the marker gave the structure its due. Built of thick chestnut post and beams in the early 1930's as a picnic shelter, it offered spectacular panoramic views of town as well as the tracks of the old Maine Central curving away into the thick Vermont woods.

The marker failed to note, however, what everyone in town knew: that it was just scary enough to test the bravery of every kid in town, or at least the foolish. Nothing but a wobbly chain-link fence, wandering tentatively along the ledge of the cliff just a yard or two from the Lookout, held the line between life and certain death. Mothers for generations had warned their kids not to press the fence, just as generations of kids had dared and doubled-dared each other to do just that.

But something was wrong.

Parker squinted to see the Lookout. He knew exactly where to focus, at the southeastern corner of the sheer face.

It wasn't there.

—∞—

He took his first trip to the Rock when he was five, piling into the family's second-hand four-door Packard, a soupy teal green which looked worse *after* it was waxed, awful colors the sad burden of buying from the available inventory off the local used car lot.

The Packard had joined his family in the declining years of its design, all rounded and soft and puffy and crowned with a hood emblem that looked like the chrome handle off some new GE appliance. Even the tires fell in line, the Packard rolling around on oversized, even bulbous, white-wall tires. The whole thing shouted *clown car*, the kind with donuts for wheels. The really fat powdered-sugar ones. His family, not the stuff of contrarians, willingly bought into the post-war program pretty much as presented by others in charge, discounted as it was. Silly cars of the left-over sort were just a part of the deal.

In the back of the car a picnic basket served as the DMZ between brother and sister, keeping a shaky peace. Both were world-class fidgets, quick to squirm and roam the tan-grey back seat which smelled like a damp rug in a cigarette factory. The Packard had hosted smokers for years, cigarettes apparently helping to win the Second World War with the good doctors giving it all a happy nod of approval.

The back seat also sported a delightful palate of intriguing stains, shouting years of kids unharnessed during family drives. He remembered a real beauty, a small handprint spilling over the edge of the driver's side seat in a fading grape-jelly-and-peanut-butter-sandwich purple, most likely Welsh's. It had been there when his dad bought the car, suggesting that other kids had roamed happily there too, well-fed—even if they, too, were gasping for fresh air.

The drive to the top of the Rock took less than half an hour—or two parental cigarettes, each, in Kent time. The picnic lunch was made from scratch: fried chicken, macaroni and potato salads, carrot sticks, and chocolate cookies, all packed neatly in a sturdy dirty-blond wicker basket along with cloth napkins, a checkered red and white tablecloth, real silverware, and a couple of thermos bottles of lemonade with maroon-red twist off caps.

And deviled eggs.

Sprinkled with paprika, the eggs were first out of the picnic basket. Deviled eggs, according to family lore, promised a horrible death if not eaten *immediately*, even if the total elapsed time from deviled-egg-production to the picnic table was less than forty-five minutes.

On that first trip to the top of the Rock his dad also took a crack at the history of the place, which was pretty close to what the marker told. In short, the place was the real deal, as was much of the promise of the American Dream back then in small towns like his across the land.

Parker Thompson had opted for the pull backwards, and that's what he was getting. He stood there, wondering if anyone still approached the picnic as a form of high family art, everything made from scratch at home and packed in those sturdy dirty-blonde wicker baskets, along with real cloth napkins, checkered red and white tablecloths, real silverware, and a thermos bottle with a red twist off cap.

And if his own kids had even seen a thermos bottle.

—⁓—

The Family Picnic Era lasted for five or six years. After that, most of his trips to the Lookout were on foot, just a bunch of kids on a goof, bikes left unlocked in the Quarry Glen at the foot of the hiking trail. But the real fun began when he could drive up there, park in a small lot at the top, and walk a gentle path down to the Lookout. It was a surprisingly romantic place, particularly if you had the gift of historical insight and imagination and could spin to a young lady a riveting tale of some scared and tired young soldier in Washington's army firing off some signal to save the day for the colonists.

But Parker Thompson did not have that gift.

What he did have was a third-hand 1957 Chevy. It had become the second family car sometime late in his seventeenth year, a slightly punch-drunk, milk-white four door tank with patched red seats and a steering wheel as large as the rims of his first bicycle. His girlfriend, a quiet junior everyone called Crickett, quickly dubbed it *The Menace*. A few years later, his father would sell *The Menace* for twenty bucks cash to a guy who had taken the bus over from Burlington, a guy so happy with his first car that he said he was going to keep it forever.

A 1957 Chevy! Twenty bucks! Parker smiled. *That guy's forever would be worth a fortune today...*

—⁂—

Late in the fall of their senior year the young couple drove to the top of the Rock, a crisp day as they walked hand-in-hand down the short path to the Lookout, the playful crunching of the leaves under their feet pleasing them both even if the colors were well-beyond their earlier golden prime. It had become their special place, talk up there unhurried and deep, and they were ready to leave their mark by carving their initials in the seasoned chestnut wood of the old structure, inside a heart.

This had been going on for generations, the whole place looking like those ancient heavy wooden tables in most college-town bars, carved to near collapse with other testaments to young love.

Another couple was up there too, which added a nice touch. Parker found a spot on a post along the south-facing side, just below eye-level, his old Boy Scout knife soon hard at work. It took a while but his effort was rewarded with a gentle kiss and an unspoken understanding that *nothing could be more forever than... well, the two of them,* their carving as sacred as those earliest writings found deep in those caves in France. It was a sweet moment, even by his fumbling standards, and marvelously in tune with the gentle tides of young love of the time, at once mysterious and innocent and forgiving.

But mostly trusting in the magic of *forever.*

—⁂—

Crickett dumped him for a Phi Gam from Colgate about twenty minutes after they both left for college, less than a year later. When he came home for Thanksgiving he slipped up to the Lookout, once again carrying his old Boy Scout knife—a habit he was about to break. It was quiet up there, and lonely, as he knew it would be. A cold late-afternoon mist was swirling around, and even he got some of those historical willies. He found the post he still thought of as *theirs*, annoyed that someone had already trespassed on their initials, the heart now looking more like a liver and the initials almost erased. Maybe he knew what he was going to do all the time, or maybe he just called an audible on the spot. He took the knife from his pocket and chipped away what was left of their initials, their *forever*. It was a crude excision, and perhaps pointless. But at that moment, high above the childhood town he had already begun to leave, he thought it an act of exquisite balance and romantic legend, like cutting off an ear but not as disfiguring.

Parker Thompson closed up his knife, ran his fingers over the old post, and tossed the knife into the cold mist.

Then he wept.

—m—

Before the storm he had always imagined he would return to the Lookout someday, taking his wife along on one of those curious journeys old men think about to discover who they were, once, and maybe even why. But sometime in the eighties—he found this out by asking around town—the Lookout was torn down and replaced by a cold concrete platform. Rumor had it that the old chestnut post and beams had gotten a little shaky, the whole thing perched too close to the eroding cliff face.

No, Parker Thompson whispered to himself, an old man adrift after a storm, *that's not what happened at all. The old structure just couldn't bear the sweet melancholy weight of all those lost forevers and broken hearts, and it collapsed of its own sad burden.*

The Custodian

He thinks about this often now—the flag and the custodian and the sounds of a radio broadcast of a baseball game on a cloudless day in April when he was not yet twelve. Or maybe it was May. His memories fray like the old cotton oxford shirts he still wears.

But when he sees the flag high atop a flagstaff, the sun catching its colors early in the morning, or later in the day when the he hears the sharp crack as a gust of wind catches it just right, it all comes back in sharp focus.

And he is sure that innocence is a glorious illusion, on loan only, and just to the young.

—∞—

His grade school was a simple red brick building, with white window and door trim and an oversize white cupola crowning the roof. He would someday tell his son it looked like the plastic school-house building on his old Lionel train set up in the basement of his home— only it was two stories tall, had a covered shed for bikes, didn't sport a plastic nail-polish-red shine, and wasn't half-eaten by a rusty-brown spaniel left home alone on a rainy day.

But the real deal, dead center on the front lawn of his school, was the flagpole.

That's just where he now stood, so vividly in his mind, ready to raise the flag at precisely 8:00 in the morning. It was 1957, and a Monday. He's quite sure of that.

Flag Duty was an honorable calling entrusted to the fifth graders. The sixth graders, having clawed their way to the top of the grade school food chain, were coasting, and everyone knew that the fourth graders were mostly morons, and it only got worse as you moved down into the lower minor leagues of his grade school. There really wasn't any training, just a quick tutorial by the custodian about half an hour before the flag-raising. It usually went well, the physics of the whole thing logical, the mechanics fairly simple, the instructions well-rehearsed.

"See?" The custodian looked at the boy. "It's easy."

"Sure." The boy wasn't, of course.

"Just don't screw it up."

"I won't, Jimmy."

The custodian seemed to like it when the kids called him by his nickname, although he was *James* at his second job at a local market, a small mom-and-pop operation where he worked three evenings a week stocking produce and most Saturdays delivering groceries, back when stores did that. The boy had seen Jimmy a couple times in the store, decked out in a snappy light-blue collared shirt, long sleeves rolled up with *Sal's Market* in a dark blue brush-script over the left pocket and *James* over the right.

"All right, then." He handed the flag to the boy. "Just one more thing. *Don't let it touch the ground. No matter what.*"

With a satisfied nod, the custodian slapped the flagpole, smiled, then headed back into the school. Jimmy walked with a slight limp, something the boy had not noticed before.

Now alone, the boy studied the grommets, feeling along the hard white canvas border, stroking the soft cotton fabric. *Yeah, this really is something.*

—⁂—

The boy took his post beside the flagpole at 7:55, fidgeted for a minute, then started to unhitch the hoisting line to begin the simple process of attaching the flag. But a breeze suddenly kicked up and the line started banging against the pole, softly at first, then more loudly, the sound magnified by the hollow flagpole and the metal clasps.

The custodian's tutorial had not included sound effects, and this was a bit unnerving. He backed off, hoping things would settle down.

They didn't.

Soon, he couldn't tame the beast, his left hand trying to steady the line, his right holding the flag which now threatened to fall to the ground.

"Don't let it touch the ground."

The boy, now thoroughly rattled, managed to force one clasp into a grommet and snap it shut. He was working on the second clasp when the line went totally nuts, the flag flying out of his hand and beginning to stream horizontally like an airport's orange wind sock, except this one was red, white and blue.

"No matter what."

Things were soon unraveling at a dizzying speed as he grabbed wildly at the hoisting line, hoping to feed another clasp into an empty grommet, his face flushing with the kind of acute embarrassment only almost-twelve-year-old boys know. Just as he feared the worst—a kind of *runaway flag* breaking away entirely and drifting its way over to the next county, a breezy frolic unimagined by the custodian, or anybody else—he snapped shut the second clasp. The breeze seemed to calm down as he quickly raised the flag up the pole, just a minute or two past 8:00…

The flag was upside-down.

The boy remembered someone telling him that this was the international signal for distress, appropriate had the school come under siege—which, as far as the custodian was concerned, it was. With arms flailing, Jimmy charged out of the school, his limp quite pronounced.

The boy was staring at the upside-down flag, and shaking. "I'm really sorry."

The custodian worked quickly and in silence to undo the damage, righting Old Glory as the boy just looked on. Turning to go back into

the school, the custodian just shook his head. The boy, roundly humili-
ated, slinked off to class in the opposite direction. There were few tender
mercies among the many humiliations visited upon the boy in his grade
school that year, but this was one: almost no one had actually seen the
disaster. Of course, as these things go, the story would soon get around.

—⁓—

When school let out that afternoon, the boy stopped by Jimmy's
basement office to offer another apology. Everyone liked the custodian, and the boy thought it the right thing to do. The door was slightly
open, and he knocked on the frosted window which had a wire mesh
insert and neat block letters which said, simply, *Custodian*.

"Jimmy?"

The custodian looked up, then waved him in. He didn't get many
visitors. The basement, by an unspoken understanding, was mostly
off-limits to the kids.

He was sitting at his desk, a battered wooden monster which had
likely entered service at the principal's office, then cycled through a
couple classrooms until landing in the custodian's office a little worse
for wear. The office, the boy saw, was really not an office at all, just an
alcove in the surprisingly high-ceilinged basement, the whole space
crowded by a massive boiler and several catwalks, one leading to a rear
exit door.

There were two windows, opened and high up the wall. They
caught the afternoon sun, along with the sounds of boys—his pals,
mostly—noisily choosing up sides on the scruffy baseball field in the
back of the school. Had anyone pressed him, he would have bet that
his best friend—a lanky, slick-fielding kid nicknamed Stretch—had
been picked first, and the noise as always was about who would take
the hapless Bauer twins, even though they claimed their third cousin
was the very Hank Bauer playing for the Yankees. A long worktable
opposite the boiler was cluttered with stuff, mostly tools and gadgets

and cleaning rags, as well as a brushed-brass work light and a small radio. A calendar—courtesy of the local Ford dealership, and featuring a well-painted picture of a handsome couple standing next to a two-tone Fairlane V-8 Sunliner convertible—hung on the wall, next to a Brooklyn Dodgers pennant. An afternoon baseball game was playing on the radio, the Dodgers hosting the Phillies. Vin Scully was doing the play-by-play.

"*Bottom of the third, no score. Cimoli, Snider and Furillo coming to the plate. Nice breeze blowing in from behind right field. Good crowd today...*"

"You like baseball?"

The boy nodded, and stammered. "Yeah, sure, but I just wanted to—"

"You a Dodgers guy?"

"You bet." The boy really wasn't, his 1956 Topps Willie Mays card stuffed into the brim of his baseball cap pledging his loyalty to the Giants. This was very tricky territory since Bobby Thomson took the pennant from the Dodgers in the bottom of the ninth just a few years before, but he figured a little good will would be in order, what with the thin ice he was on.

The custodian smiled. "Dodgers got a two-run lead heading into the third. Roger Craig's pitching strong today." The boy, oddly, would always remember that detail, along with the hum of the Vin Scully play-by-play.

"*The F. & M. Schaefer Brewing Company delighted to bring you the game today. Schaefer Beer, the one to have when having more than one...*"

The custodian's desk was neat, empty but for a few technical manuals, a stack of orange invoices, and a crumpled bag of potato chips. A framed black and white photograph sat at the edge, almost precisely in the center of the desk: three soldiers—all unshaven, their eyes hollow, a heavy bandage around the forehead of the guy on the right, who was smoking a cigarette—were sitting on a tank, its treads caked in mud, the gun turret smashed. They were holding an American flag.

"*Breeze still blowing in from right, picking up a bit...*"

The custodian saw the boy looking at the photo. "That was towards the end of the war, in a little town somewhere in France."

"*Snider takes one on the inside corner. Bill Jackowski calling them behind the plate today. Don't forget to get those Lucky Strikes…*"

"That's me in the middle, the others my best buddies in the platoon." He paused. "I was the oldest, and they called me Pops." He smiled. "I was twenty-four."

"*Hearn, joining 'em this year, on the mound for the Phillies. Touches the brim of his cap, shakes off a call…*"

"The guy on the left—just a kid from some small town in Iowa—played ball at Carolina. Talked about going back to his high school and coaching after the war."

"*Here's the fastball, Snider leaning in. Strike two called. You Dodger fans may remember that Hearn pitched a few years for the Giants, the tall right-hander handing us a 3-1 defeat in game one of that 1951 pennant play-off series…*"

The custodian smiled. "We talked baseball all the time you know, over there."

"*Couple big doubleheaders coming up at Ebbets…*"

The custodian reached over and moved the picture a few inches.

"But he never made it home, blown up a couple weeks after this photo was taken." The custodian paused. "I took some shrapnel in the leg, just below the knee, the same day." He reached over to the radio and turned the volume down, his hand moving the dial slowly, carefully, then looked at the boy.

"The flag tells his story, and it tells my story, and it tells the stories of millions of other guys, guys just like us."

It was very quiet, the boy remembers.

"You see, son, that's the thing." The custodian paused again. "That's… that's the thing about our flag."

The custodian looked away, but just for a moment, then turned and smiled, although it was a sad one, that's what the boy thought.

"But you didn't let it touch the ground, did you?"

—⦿—

The boy rode his bike to school early the next morning, taking the longer route—the one with a tempting down-hill run, just past the old railroad coal siding. He could take both hands off the handlebars for almost half a minute, and listen to the *ratta-tatta-tatta* sounds of a baseball card flapping against the spokes of his back wheel, rigged with a clothespin like all the boys did. When he got to school and parked his bike he pretended to fuss with the clothespin, but really he just wanted to watch another fifth grader handle the flag duty. A pretty red-head in a bright green dress with yellow flowers—sunflowers, he guessed—was listening to the custodian's tutorial, just as he had done the day before.

He liked her. She had moved into town in the beginning of the year, and sat two rows ahead of him—and she seemed to like him, at least sometimes. He watched the custodian finish his tutorial, slapping the flagpole as he left the redhead to her duties. Within minutes she had raised the flag smartly, even in the breeze, and that made him happy. In class that morning he told her what a nice job she had done. She said thank you, with a look that was curious but not unkind.

—⦿—

Every so often that spring the boy stopped by the custodian's office to talk baseball, and again the next fall, and on into the next spring—his last before graduating from sixth grade and heading off to middle school. The boy made his last visit to the basement on a muggy day in early June. Goodbyes were something new for the boy, and change was everywhere that spring of 1958: the redhead told him she was moving again, to Texas, but would write; his dog took off one day never to return; his dad lost his job… and both the Giants and Dodgers left them all, moving to their new homes on the West Coast.

Summers would never be the same.

As the boy looked around the basement for the last time, he noticed that the custodian's radio was playing music, and the Dodgers pennant was nowhere to be seen.

The Redeye Home

—〰—

"It's time."

The voice was deep, Kentucky-bred, and whiskey-cured. It was not unkind, although Thomas Brannon sensed some brusqueness in his father's next words.

"You need to come home, son."

His mother had said the same thing only hours ago.

Or was it more?

Her voice was still Georgia-sweet, soft like the dusty red clay in the late summer when the rains didn't come. But in it he sensed something else.

Was it forgiveness?

Thomas felt something—a heaviness—lift from his shoulders, and he struggled to remember just what that something could be.

—⁘—

His mother was raised outside the tiny town of Mustard's Redoubt, Georgia. Shy and always tall for her age, Jessie Pettie had a gift for music. By the time she was fourteen she had become the assistant choral director at the First Reformed Church of the Redeemer, where her father—raised on the strong stuff of what he called *the old time religion* and preaching a noisy brand of muscular Christianity—was Pastor and her mother led the twice-weekly Bible study group.

Her parents had met as students at Blue Mountain Bible College near Tupelo, and both had hoped that she would follow them there for college, and then into the ministry. But Jesse's calling was the softer soul-soothing message of song, and she followed her muse to a small junior college outside Boston when she was not quite eighteen. In the spring of her second year she met Jack Brannon on a blind date to a Red Sox game at Fenway. A hard-partying kid on a full football boat-ride to Boston College, he had been raised around the soul-crushing strip mines of Eastern Kentucky.

If not quite love at first sight, she would tell Thomas, *it started to click at the bottom of the eighth, the Sox up by three.* His father, Thomas remembered, would always correct her by claiming she was *all in* by the top of the sixth.

They were married in the fall, a slightly mis-matched but loving couple who decided to call Boston their home. Thomas was born a year later, and a sister, Gwen, two years after that. Thomas would have said it was a happy home, and he would be right. Jack Brannon coached football and taught early American history at Newton Academy and Jessie taught music in the Belmont School District, mostly in the gifted programs. Thomas followed his dad to Boston College, where he played tight end, taking an assistant coaching job at a small college near Albuquerque after graduation.

And if he thought about this at all, he was not a young man unduly burdened by much of anything. Although a recent engagement to a lanky tennis coach at New Mexico State College had cratered, his disappointments in his twenty-four years were hardly the stuff of tragedy. He was a generous soul, easy to friend, with trespasses mild and blundering rather than malicious. And with his recent break-up, he had tried to make a real effort to pay a little more attention to his parents back home.

Yeah, Thomas thought, *a quick visit back home. That's what I need.*
But he couldn't shake a feeling that something was *off.*
Can't pin it down, but something slipping, since... yes, since... what?
He felt some stutters in his memory. More awkward than really

alarming, it was not the big stuff, but the little things—last names mashed up with the wrong first names, dates and details floating around, adrift and fuzzy. He had this gnawing sense that he had left something *undone*, like the dreams he remembered having in college about a class he had failed to attend, or a bill left unopened on his desk.

What was the book my mother wanted?

When were the Yankees coming into Fenway for a five-game series? Was it next weekend, or the end of the month? A couple tickets for his mom and dad—third base side, low to the field. Yeah, that's where they sat the night they met—that's the ticket.

And those airline... things. The... points. American? United? Yes. United.

Thomas relaxed.

I got plenty for a red-eye one-stop into Logan, even for just a few days' visit.

—✳—

Thomas sat alone at Gate 14A, watching the 757 pull into the gate, its graceful nose catching the last colors of a blood-red desert sunset, the large tail fin sporting the new colors of the carrier's merger with Continental.

He was always early to an airport, but as he looked around the boarding gate it was quiet even for a Tuesday night redeye out of Albuquerque. He nodded to an older couple sitting a few rows away on the hard-plastic departure seats. Their quiet banter reminded him of the way his mom and dad always traveled, and he smiled. A twenty-something raced down the nearly empty concourse, her backpack ajar, trying to make her boarding for the Frontier hop to Phoenix at the gate next door. The boarding attendant, in a snappy blazer and an end-of-shift mood, just shook his head but held the jet-way door open, with a quick ticket check and a shrug. As she boarded, the girl glanced back at Thomas. Her blue eyes were half hidden under a worn cardinal-red

Chi Omega cap, and her long hair poked out the back in a braided ponytail, matching the straw-yellow of her sorority's Greek letters.

Go Owls, he said to himself, his sister having been a Chi Omega too. He smiled as she gave him a thumbs-up, then disappeared into the plane.

Soon, he saw that nothing was left on the departure board but United 893, his one-stop to Boston through Philadelphia. It showed a 9:55 on-time departure.

Good.

Thomas thought he would buy his mother a book—he still couldn't remember the one she wanted to read—before boarding, and maybe grab a quick bite to eat. He looked down the concourse for the bookstore, sure it was in the hub connecting the A and B concourses, close to the food court. He could almost taste the soft-crusted by-the-slice Sbarro pizza he liked, easy on the pepperoni, always.

Damn I'm hungry.

But both the book store and pizza, much to his surprise, were no longer there.

Guess they're in the B concourse, he thought. *I'll get the book in Philadelphia, maybe a quick Egg McMuffin there too.*

He suddenly felt cold.

Should be someplace during the stopover to buy a Phillies windbreaker, he thought. *If I've got time.*

—❧—

Thomas felt the slight jolt as the plane lifted off, a few minutes behind schedule. It banked gracefully into its slow turn away from the faint streaks of emerald-green and light blue left in the long-retreat of the western early summer sky. They climbed through a little chop, then leveled off for the four-hour flight. Thomas enjoyed flying, and he quickly settled in. He absently watched the two flight attendants gently close the half-curtain behind them as they moved into mid-cabin economy, dim ming the lights. Thomas caught the eye of the younger one, about his age. Her thick auburn hair, cut in an impish bob with the shine of a pedigreed Irish setter, reminded him of his almost-bride. She nodded toward the closed curtain, then smiled with a *maybe next time* shrug.

How fitting, he thought.

When she got to Thomas, she pulled a small courtesy blanket from the overhead and dropped it gently on to his lap.

"Where're you headed?" she whispered, kindly. Her voice was unhurried, *Tammie Moriarity* stitched in bright gold script letters on her uniform blouse, just below her wings.

"Boston." Thomas paused, then smiled. "Home."

He thought about adding a little more, but didn't. He nodded, and then simply thanked her. As she walked away, his mind began to drift with the rhythmic hum of the cabin, as soothing as the soft lullabies he remembered his mother singing to him as a child.

—ɷ—

"Soon now."

The voice seemed oddly familiar, but gauzy, washing in from somewhere over his right shoulder. He turned his neck, but saw only the backside of the bobbed-haired flight attendant, heading toward the rear cabin. Then, without turning around, she held both arms out, palms up and shrugged.

"Odd," Thomas thought.

Just then he felt the giant plane nose up, the two Pratt & Whitney turbofan jet engines racing as the plane began to climb, gently at first, then more hungrily into the night sky. He looked out his window, but could see nothing but moon-soaked white clouds outside, brushed with silver. He couldn't shake his chill, and was about to ask for another soft blanket when the cockpit intercom clicked on.

"Good evening, ladies and gentlemen, this is your First Officer speaking."

His voice was the one practiced by all pilots, a kind of cowboy folksy, *aw shucks* rhythm suggesting it's all just an easy West Texas evening country-lane drive up here. "Sorry to bother you." There was a click, then silence for a few seconds, then another click. "Captain Anne Esposito is kinda… uh… busy right now, so she's asked me to give you a little update. We're gonna have to go around a patch of turbulence just up ahead, so we're gonna be… uh… a little late into Philadelphia. But we should make it up on our shorter leg on into Boston. Tammie Moriarity tells us they got you all set for the night back there, so you might want to go ahead and set your watches ahead now. We do that up here, and it's… uh… going on 1:08 Eastern."

The plane suddenly bucked, but not alarmingly. "Be sure you're buckled in, seat belt secure. While we don't expect anything too—"

A blinding flash exploded outside his window, the plane rocking hard to the left, then dipping sharply to the right. Thomas heard a scream in the back, and saw the older attendant sprawled out on the cabin floor, a beverage cart broken and twisted against her. As she tried to get up, the plane dipped again, and Thomas saw the blood on her pale blue slacks, an expanding dark island of maroon.

No, no, no… Not again. Thomas felt himself scream, but wasn't sure anything had actually come out.

Thomas tried to unbuckle his belt.

I can't feel my hands.

The plane suddenly heeled over, the man two rows forward on the aisle—*that nice older man from the terminal with his wife,* Thomas thought—came flying out of his seat. Thomas, on instinct, tried to reach out to him.

I can save him.

But his arms—*why won't they **MOVE**?*—useless as Thomas saw the man's neck catch the popped door of the overhead with a sickening crack, things tumbling out of the bin, everything falling—*things suddenly so cold*—and floating—*that thing, it was—I REMEMBER IT ALL NOW… it was an accident, a car accident, I couldn't—*the plane in a straight dive now—*the alarms, the alarms, where were they all coming from—?"*

—ↄɔ—

The night nurse had just finished her second cup of coffee and was about to catch up on some paperwork when the bio-monitor alarms on her console went off.

"HE'S CRASHING IN 14A!" she shouted to the young attending, a pup just out of his residency at Mass General who was trying to catch a duty-nap on the lumpy cot in the darkened room just to her left. She grabbed one of the three charts on her desk, and they both raced to the room.

"This the guy they brought in with both his parents?"

The nurse nodded. "Brannon. Thomas Joseph Brannon."

"I lost his mom downstairs in Trauma A, what, eight days ago now? A mess, nothing I could do. Dad DOA. Bad scene." As they entered the room, the doctor turned to the nurse. "Any directive here?" He looked at her tag. "Ms. Moriarity."

"His sister came in two days ago, flew in from somewhere out west. She had his insurance stuff, a notarized directive—*nothing heroic in the event*—well, you know the drill, doctor." She paused. "Legal cleared it. Patient's been on the ventilator, feeding tube, both arms crushed at the scene, nearly bled out you know..."

The nurse realized how harsh, how *clinical*, that sounded. She felt for the small crucifix she had worn discretely for years as the doctor went to work, whatever that meant now. "EMT's told me he was driving his mother and father home from the Fenway. Wet highway, lost control."

The doctor studied the charts, then moved deliberately around Thomas Joseph Brannon. The room grew quieter at each of his studied movements, machines and monitors soon falling silent, bright bouncy lines sliding first into chop, then into the flat, then dark to nothing. He looked at his watch, and then the nurse. "I'm calling it. 1:08."

—꿈—

The young doctor closed the door to room 14W, now empty and quiet. This, for him, was the hardest part, and he needed a moment. He had yet to understand the idea of endings, or the even greater mystery of death, and wondered if he ever would. He paused by the window at the end of his floor and stood there, silently watching a silver-white cloud brush past the bright moon, mid-sky above the sleeping city below.

The Caretaker's Whispers

This is what the caretaker knows:

The dusty saloons down by the wharf—where the men drink their whiskey hard, and look you in the eye straight—are where the saddest stories are told. But you have to listen, and listen carefully, and mostly to what is not said.

And this is what the caretaker sees:

The cemetery sits high on a bluff along a wide bend in the Mississippi. Its wrought iron entrance gates—crowded by the trunks of the two magnolia trees standing guard on either side—are pitted, broken, and rusted open. One gate has slipped entirely off its hinges, and now leans against its guardian tree. This is of little matter since the gates to the cemetery have not been closed in years, now dug deep into the soil, and he wonders if the new caretaker will set them free.

And this is what the caretaker believes:

It is the fading light of the day long gone, the sorrows of the re-membered undressing in the night, and the hushed voices of the buried—they have whispered to him for years—that are the special burden of the caretaker. But he has learned to listen to the whispers, generously and without judgment.

About all the rest, he can only wonder.

He has lived in the cemetery's tidy two-bedroom caretaker's cottage for much of his life now, but he will soon leave it. It rests atop a shady knoll deep in the left corner of the cemetery. Prickly clumps of Spanish moss, draped over the gnarled branches of several live oaks, sway in the breeze rolling over from the fertile lowlands across the river. The clumps are thickest on the smaller end branches, and these are the ones that seem to be dead, although they might not be. He has been told for years that the moss does not choke the tree, and that the oaks, the gray moss, and the resurrection fern which weaves itself around both the branches and the moss live in perfect harmony.

He would like to believe that, although he is no longer sure.

The roof, long tickled by the moss, is patched now, and he remembers when he and his young bride replaced the old tar shingles with sheets of smoke-scarred tin. Two coats of glossy forest green once worked their magic on the roof, the tin salvaged from the fire at the old feed store outside town which took the life of Old Man McNichols, one of seven McNichols buried in the cemetery.

But that was long ago.

The roof is now faded to a flat and dusty pond green, and the caretaker now lives by himself, his wife of many years slipping quietly away one night a year ago. Although he had been given a small family plot toward the front of the cemetery, she had always told her husband that she wished to be buried closer to the cottage, and that's where she rests. It was a loving marriage, and her whispers are the softest in the night. They are also the hardest, he would tell you, and they rest heaviest on his shoulders.

—⁂—

Behind the cottage is a stepped gravel walkway leading up to three well-maintained sheds.

Two resemble the slant-roofed and open-fronted wooden produce stands which cluster a mile out of town on the two-lane to White Apple Springs. Tractors, heavy digging equipment, and a seven-year-old Jeep are neatly parked in one; smaller equipment fills the second.

The front of the third shed—the smallest—is covered by a heavy white canvas flap with a clear plastic window, slightly off-centered. The caretaker found it at a surplus store in Jackson, what was left of a larger wedding tent. He ties it down at night and in bad weather, and rolls it up smartly when the weather is good. Inside, a poured concrete floor is painted a light gray, the finished walls a soft vanilla-yellow, and a large fan with a frosted globe light hangs from the ceiling. The structure is surprisingly well-insulated, although the caretaker runs a small electric heater in the winter and a de-humidifier in the summer. A paper map of the cemetery grounds runs six feet along the back wall, and is covered by a sheet of thin plexiglass which has started to yellow and crack along the corners. Two thick-legged tables, built of oak stained a rich fawn-brown, sit in the middle of the floor. Each holds a large glass-top display case, the shallow kind found hosting the curious stuff of libraries and museums and flea markets everywhere.

The first case hosts a directory of those buried in the cemetery, cross-referenced to the grids on the map. That case is never locked, but seldom opened anyway: most folks who visit the cemetery are the folks in town, and they know their way around. The directory is page-worn, and will—the caretaker has been told this—soon be replaced by a kiosk at the entrance to the cemetery.

The second display case is locked. The idea for this case came to the caretaker's wife when she found an old trunk in the attic of their cottage in the second year of their marriage. In it were dozens of the trailing scraps of the lives of people buried in the cemetery, things the couple guessed had been left over the years on the graves themselves, or slipped under the caretaker's door, or even sent in mailers from places far away.

Among the items she found was the stained deed to the old Grayson Hotel, which was lost to a gambling debt in the spring of 1897 just four months before it burned to the ground. Sixteen Graysons are buried in a far corner of the cemetery under a specimen oak.

There were the pistols which once belonged to the Haslett brothers, ornate small caliber Colts with their initials engraved on the handles, gifted to them by their father. The brothers are buried facing each other, under weathered headstones with the same date of April 23, 1906. Nine Hasletts rest near the center of the cemetery.

There was the wrinkled page from a 1923 Ole Miss football program, a raw-boned and leather-helmeted tight end named Aaron Whittingham smiling for the photographer just hours before his appendix burst on the practice field early in the season. Twelve Whittinghams are buried in the cemetery, and Aaron is buried next to his mother and father and his five sisters, close by the bluff.

And there was the letter left by Mary Anne Nobles on the tiny grave marker of her son, who was just two when he was laid to rest on September 18, 1918. The note was yellowed and stained and sad, asking the boy's forgiveness in a careful script. Sixteen Nobles are buried around the tiny marker for Curtis Alexander Nobles, but not Mary Anne. She left town the night she placed the letter on the grave. At least that's what the men in the saloons down by the wharf will tell you.

No one seems to know where she went.

—⁂—

The caretaker and his wife soon bought the second case for the shed from a jeweler in town, then spent months choosing what things to display in it.

They knew that these would not be the things of interest to the chatty tourists who spill into town from the Trace Parkway in the spring, only a few of whom wander into the shed anyway. They come from Ohio and Michigan and Maine, packed two-by-two in sleek luxury buses looking for the two-or-three-grooved bullets which once littered the bloodied fields on the outskirts of town, or the gray tunic a young Confederate officer wore as he left his trembling bride on the steps of some home built on a land grant signed by Martin Van Buren, or the tools left behind by skilled craftsmen who had come down from New York or Pennsylvania to work on a planter's home, only to flee North at the beginning of the War.

Bullets and tunics and rusty tools, the caretaker tells them, are the kinds of things that fill the two historic museums in town, as well as many of the old family homes too. There, he tells them—and not in his shed—can be found the sorrows and burdens of history writ large.

No, it is only the sorrows writ small that he tenders in his shed. They are the sorrows that whisper to the caretaker at night, and they are the special burden he carries—a burden which came along soon after he arrived in Moultre Landing, Mississippi, years ago.

—m—

The *Molly Moran*—a hard-working tug pushing a heavy barge-load of cement up to Vicksburg—was already sixteen miles up-river from Moultre Landing before Cade LeMonte opened his eyes. The morning was damp, the sun already burning off a haze, and he knew he was still half drunk.

What he didn't know was where he was, although he knew where he wasn't—his cramped bunk on the old tug, port-side deck two, directly above that of his pal Crisper Dietz. Where he *was,* was tangled up in a moldy wool blanket, and curled up on a damp hard-planked floor. A lump was crumpled under an old raincoat at his feet, under a neon sign hanging crookedly on the wall which said The Pegged Leg, although the *P* was missing. The lump smelled of cheap whiskey and stale beer too, and it was snoring.

"Crisper?"

He and Crisper grew up poor in Bayou Blue, Louisiana, a tiny shrimping village along the Gulf Coast. When they were both eighteen they left to find work on the tugs and barges and docks from New Orleans to Mobile, and signed on to the *Molly Moran* in April of 1934. They had been working hard on the tug for only a few months when it pulled alongside the Landing's wharf the day before, and both boys, their pockets stuffed with five weeks of cash wages, swapped the duty with two other crewmen for an evening off the boat.

That night, they did their first real river-drinking.

The evening started out quietly enough, with a few beers and the catfish dinner special at a place a short walk up the steep road from the wharf, in the center of town. But trouble soon found them when the boys walked back down that steep road and over a few blocks to a tough section of the wharf. Six saloons of questionable virtue wound along a single block which hugged a slight bend in the river, and it was in The Pegged Leg that the devil-rum took the boys hard that night, and a little back-room poker did the rest.

Cade rubbed his temples, then kicked the lump at his feet. "That better be you, Crisper."

"Whaaa—?"

"The time, man. What *time* is it?"

"I dunno." Crisper uncrumpled from the raincoat, slowly. Crisper wore a watch. "*Shit.*"

—⚭—

The caretaker thinks often of that morning: how the *Molly Moran* left the two of them behind, $34.78 between them in their pockets, two scared young men smelling of whiskey and shame and defeat, their lives skidding on the mischiefs of men in the night.

But he also thinks of this: lives that skid on the mischiefs of men in the night can also find grace in the smile of a good woman in the morning.

That $34.78 was enough for them to find a room at a cheap boarding house on the wharf for a week, clean up, and get something to eat. They decided to try a small breakfast-and-brunch restaurant back up on the bluff, and begin figuring things out from there. The walk did both of them some good, and they took a table toward the back of Mama's Place.

"Breakfast or brunch?" The waitress waved two menus in the air, and nodded to the clock on the wall, which read 11:28. "You're right on the line." She smiled. "For about another two minutes." A name tag on her blouse said Violette, her soft voice said kind. "Look, I probably shouldn't let you in on all Mama's little secrets, but go for the breakfast menu." She lowered her voice to a whisper. "It's cheaper, and pretty much the same stuff." She shrugged. "Except you don't get a complimentary Bloody Mary." She winked. "Maybe that's not such a bad thing for you two this morning?"

Cade LaMonte laughed. He liked her. "No, not a bad thing this morning. Maybe not a bad thing *ever*." He took the menu and ordered a couple eggs over easy with toast. Crisper jumped in with his order, a plain three egg omelet with an extra order of cornbread. On the river Crisper often talked about *his* mama's *cohnbread* growing up, and when Violette brought their breakfast she had stacked the basket of cornbread high.

That morning, Cade LaMonte had a feeling that things were going to turn out just fine in Moultre Landing, Mississippi.

—◊—

Within a few days Cade found a part-time job on the wharf, Crisper a full-time job in the kitchen of the old Hotel Jefferson, near the town's train depot. They made enough to pay their rent, buy some fresh clothes, and even spring for the Sunday brunch at Mama's Place. Cade liked the place for Violette, Crisper for the food, and both of them for the extra cornbread always gifted on the house. And it was at breakfast there one morning that Brett Moultre changed their lives.

Brett, a popular mayor running for a fourth term, had been chatting it up with folks all over town for weeks, mostly about jobs. He had heard talk the two young men were hard workers who made friends easily, and had never again set foot in The Pegged Leg.

Yes, Brett Moultre liked what he saw. Especially in Cade LaMonte.

He also liked what a little political magic could do in a small-town election. The town cemetery needed a digger, Cade needed a steady job, and the mayor was just the man to stitch it all together on a hand-shake and a promise by the young man to cork the devil rum, and be good to that nice young waitress over at Mama's Place.

—∞—

The new digger worked hard, and just after his twenty-third birth-day was appointed caretaker, the youngest in town history. He moved into the cottage with Violette, who had become his wife a year before, and two years later they welcomed a daughter, Coraline Mae.

Laughter soon filled the days.

And when Coraline was still young and silly and loved to chase the evening bugs, she would tag along with the caretaker as he closed the gates to the cemetery at dusk, back when the gates still worked.

"They're not goin' anywhere, papa," Coraline would say, then giggle. Her eyes were bright with the innocence of the very young, her pigtails tied with yellow ribbons, her favorite color.

And then she would take her father's hand as they walked back to the cottage, under and around the sweet olive and the oak, and they would talk in the special way of fathers and daughters—of dreams and hopes, and how silly the boys can be. But only rarely of death, and that always with special care.

"I know you tell Mama you hear the whispers, late in the night," she once told him when she was nine. *"But I never do."*

The caretaker then cupped his ear, and tilted his head in the direc-tion of the river.

"Better you hear the songs of the river," he said to her gently.

And back when the gates still worked, the local kids would fol-low Coraline home to the cemetery, to climb on the gates and ride and swing and laugh and dream of the things they didn't have and the places many knew, even then, they may never see. The caretaker would chase them away, but never too quickly and always with a quick wink to his daughter. The two of them would then share a quiet confidence that she would be one of the luckier ones, the wider world beyond the bluff opening to her, someday.

—⁂—

At exactly eight in the morning, on the first Tuesday of August in the troubled year of 1969, the caretaker carefully raised five flags—the Spanish, the French, the British, the Confederate, and the American— on poles set in a row just to the left of his cottage. In their time, each flag had flown over the town, making its claim for the allegiance of its people. The American flag was always the first one he raised, centered on a taller pole. The four other flags—to its left and right—flapped lazily in the breeze, tethered to a past they no longer owned.

But this was not what the caretaker was thinking about: the ground around the cemetery had turned soft over the last four days—a soaking rain in from the Coast had swooped into the Deep South, flash-flooding up-river—and there was a new grave for the caretaker to prepare.

But it would be done right, as they always were. Even in the wettest weather.

And it would likely be his last, although only he and his daughter—a commercial artist now living in Chicago, happily married with twin girls—knew that.

—⁂—

"It's gonna be late, papa."

The caretaker's daughter pointed to the clock above the open window of the ticket counter, next to the chalkboard where the agent had carefully written the schedule for the day, June 24, 1951.

"Nope, not today." The caretaker grinned. "Wanna bet?"

Coraline and her father stood on the concrete platform of the Moultre Landing train station, waiting for the northbound *Gulf Coast Special* to roll into town on its way to St. Louis with connections to

Chicago. The train was scheduled to arrive at 5:25 in the evening, and it was already 5:18 with no sign of the two Alco diesels—each in the distinctive two-tone maroon and red of the Gulf, Mobile & Western Mississippi Railroad Company—tip-toeing over the old wooden trestle half a mile out of town and blowing its horn as it rounded a last graceful curve on the single track mainline.

"I'm in, papa. The usual?"

"The usual, girl."

Both could already taste victory.

The caretaker and his daughter would come into town at least once a week to watch the *Special* glide in, always standing where the dining car—in the middle of the nine-car train—would crawl to a stop, but not always. This evening they smiled when the dining car stopped right in front of them, then waved to the folks seated for the early dinner. An enormous man soon stepped off the diner, wearing the distinctive loose-fitting gray pants of the dining car cook and a bright red bandana around his neck.

"Evening, Crisper!" The greeting by the caretaker and his daughter was quick and warm and shouted out in sweet harmony.

"Y'all doing?" The voice was deep, smoky, and kind, his grin wide and warm.

"Doin' fine, jus' like always." Coraline smiled, and the caretaker nodded, approvingly.

"Bet you been makin' more of them little glazed-clay figures, that's what I'm guessin."

Crisper had signed on with the railroad right after Cade married Violette, working his way up to the dining cars on the Gulf line. He was always a welcomed visitor to the cottage and on a recent visit he noticed dozens of clay figures—little trolls and unicorns and spotted ponies—lined up on the mantle above the large hearth in the cottage's cozy living room. Coraline had been learning to kiln-dry and glaze the tiny figures in an arts class, and she had gifted him a bright yellow unicorn the year before.

She just shrugged, but the caretaker jumped right in. "Coraline won a second-place in the county art fair this spring." He smiled. "Mighty proud of her, we are. Her eye for art, that's her ticket, Crisper, her gift. It'll take her places, and far. I just know it."

Crisper enjoyed his life on the rails. He would talk, in the light of a fire in that cozy cottage, of the legendary chicken pie on the Wabash *Banner Blue*, and the fresh Gulf shellfish gumbo, crab fingers and dinner-sized bottle of Bertolli on the varnish of the Illinois Central, and the crisp cotton sheets in the drawing rooms of the Southern *Crescent*, neatly dressed by the porters whom he knew by name. He told tales of the time he worked the *Gulf Coast Rebel* on the GM&O out of Mobile just so he could visit a special girl in Artesia, Mississippi, and the summer he rode the *Ann Rutledge* all the way to St. Louis just to see the Arch.

And if anyone suggested that his own Gulf, Mobile & Western Mississippi Railroad Company didn't quite have the stuff of the rival railroads serving the South, he would tell them that *his hot buttered cohnbread,* fresh from the oven of his dining car, the *Bayou Belle,* was the best on the rails.

"You cookin' for a full house in the *Bayou Belle* this evening, Crisper?"

Crisper smiled. "Got a few empty seats at the first seating, Coraline Mae." This was always part of the fun, watching him break into a big grin. "So it looks like the great Gulf, Mobile & Western Mississippi Railroad Company baked a little too much somethin' again this afternoon, young lady." As the *Special* blew its horn twice, he reached into his pocket and handed her three thick slices of his hot-buttered specialty, wrapped in a napkin warm to the touch. As he hopped back on the train, he turned back to her. "You win the bet tonight?"

Coraline held the cornbread high, and smiled.

"Well, you leave a slice for your papa's supper anyway, girl."

—ɯ—

Brett Moultre stood on a temporary wooden stand, raised three feet above the cracked platform of the train depot. The platform was decked out in red, white and blue bunting left over from the town's Fourth of July parade, and it was bowed in the middle where he was joined by three members of the town council, the local school superintendent, and twelve members of the high school band.

Scattered along the platform were locals come to see the last run of the *Gulf Coast Special,* although Brett was disappointed that fewer than two dozen had shown to bid a farewell worthy of an old friend. Only four passengers were ready to board the train: a young couple in tie-dyed jeans, likely off to Memphis State; a middle-aged man with the tired look of a traveling salesman in a slump; and an older man in a slightly worn but well-pressed dark brown suit, starched white shirt and wide tie in a cream and maroon pattern of the late forties. His shoes, well-shined lace-ups, looked new and maybe a bit uncomfortable. The man held a spotless dark brown fedora in his left hand close against his thigh, and the right hand, hanging loosely at his side, trembled. In his suit coat pocket was a one-way ticket on the *Gulf Coast Special* to St. Louis, with connections to Chicago on the Illinois Central.

Two strapped suitcases—not a single travel sticker affixed—sat on a wooden cart at the front end of the platform waiting to be loaded on the baggage car. Most people on the platform knew the suitcases belonged to the caretaker, and that he was about to say goodbye to Moultre Landing.

Two weeks before Labor Day, he had asked Brett to meet him for breakfast at Mama's Place. The caretaker, who had buried three Moultres himself, told his friend that it was simply time for him to go, that he had worked hard for almost forty years and wanted to spend what time he had left with his daughter and two grandchildren in their home outside Chicago.

The two of them talked, as old men along the river do, of their younger days along the bluff, and of friends and kin gone and time too, and the footsteps they sensed behind them. What they didn't talk about was the kindness shown a young man and his friend so many years ago: they didn't need to.

A few days later, the caretaker found a plain envelope tacked to the door of the cottage. In it was a first-class railroad ticket, a deluxe bedroom on the *Gulf Coast Special* through-sleeper all the way to Chicago, the *Bayou View*. There was no note, other than an announcement, handsomely engraved on a cream-colored stock and signed by the president of the Gulf, Mobile & Western Mississippi Railroad Company, that the *Gulf Coast Special* would make its last run through town on September 23, 1969.

—∞—

With two short blasts, the *Special* inched forward, picking up speed slowly as it cleared the platform of the depot for the last time. The caretaker pressed against the window of his sleeper, and he saw that Brett Moultre seemed to be looking for his friend. The caretaker tapped on his window, and saw that his friend had seen him. They both smiled.

The caretaker decided on the second seating for dinner, and settled into his stuffed chair as the train swayed gently on its last run up to Vicksburg. He closed his eyes and thought of magical summers of evening bugs and glazed yellow unicorns and the hot buttered *cohnbread* of the great Gulf, Mobile & West Mississippi Railroad Company, and all the many souls he had buried in his cemetery.

The last, not two months earlier, had been one of the hardest, his friend Crisper Dietz.

Later that night, after the porter had pulled his berth and turned down its fine cotton sheets, the caretaker listened to the sound of the rails, and drifted to sleep. And in the morning, somewhere north of Memphis, the caretaker awakened, and realized that he no longer hears the whispers, and he smiled.

—∞—

The dusty saloons by the wharf—where the river men once drank their whiskey hard and looked you straight in the eye, and where two young boys from the tiny shrimping village of Bayou Blue, Louisiana, once found their destiny—are fewer now, mostly morphed into tony wine bars and coffee shops and a vegan bistro. These are the places where the tired tourists sit, silently tapping away on their smartphones.

Mama's Place is gone, too, a tony French bakery in its place.

The cemetery still sits high on the bluff, although erosion along the wide bend in the river has recently taken a chunk of bluff less than half a mile away. Glossy black gates once again swing freely, next to a kiosk at the entrance with its new digital directory. The two magnolia trees still stand guard, and the caretaker's cottage has another new tin roof, as well as a second headstone next to that of Violette LaMonte. The new caretaker takes special care of those, brushing them off every morning after he hoists the flags, just four of them now.

And tucked away in the corner of the wooden display case in the shed is a dinner menu from the *Bayou Belle* dining car, an engraved card from the President of the Gulf, Mobile & Western Mississippi Railroad Company announcing the last run of the *Gulf Coast Special* on September 23, 1969, and a crumpled ticket on a through-sleeper to Chicago issued to a Mr. Cade LaMonte of Moultre Landing, Mississippi.

Slim Chance

"Mister... ah... *Mister Bickford.*"

Maryellen Olsen, Assistant Professor of Law, looked up from her seating chart, then out towards the bleacher seats in the large, semicircular classroom on the first floor of Roberts Hall, hoping one Thomas Aquinas Bickford III would heed the call.

The oversize double-hung windows in the back of the room were open, a gentle breeze blowing across the leafy quad—and with it the soft sounds of a James Taylor track. She was sure it was from his *Mud Slide Slim and the Blue Horizon* album, and even she would concede it was coming from a happier place than her *Basic Principles of Administrative Law I,* probably the Theta house a block away. A true Taylor fan since she and a couple of her friends piled into an old VW van and drove sixteen hours to Tacoma, Washington, for the 1969 Sky River Rock Festival, she also could feel the campus beginning to come alive with the promise of the first real spring weekend of the semester, most everyone finished with their Friday classes.

Except first-year law students, taught by junior faculty.

And Maryellen Olsen was just five years out of Vanderbilt Law, a much sought-after Fifth Circuit Court of Appeals clerkship burnishing her already impressive resume, her classes noted for her rigorous discipline and sharp-edged wit.

Mister Bickford, in his first year of law school, had yet to burnish much of anything, although he certainly understood the idea of academic rigor, along with its noble intent.

Spring, however, had come early, and he was sitting close by the open windows high up in the bleacher seats, where some twenty minutes earlier he had quietly untethered himself from the professor's lecture, dialing into that very promise of a warm spring college weekend. He had come to the study of law later than many of his classmates after two notably casual years as a failed low minor leagues baseball player, and three as an Outward-Bound guide along the Colorado River. The luxurious moustache he had grown since his official student picture—the one pasted in Professor Olsen's notebook—had served for months as a useful camouflage. At least until now.

"Professor?"

"Mr. Bickford, would you care to enlighten us with an answer to my question?"

Well, of course I would be delighted to do just that, Professor, if only I had heard what it was.

"Ahh… could you repeat the question?" *Don't do it.* "Please?"

Shit.

He had seen real lawyers—at least real *television* lawyers—jockey to buy a little time too, although maybe they didn't roll over with that *please* stuff.

"Of course, Mr. Bickford." The professor looked down at her notes, then up to the bleachers. "May I assume you are familiar with the idea of due process under the Fourteenth Amendment?" Thomas nodded knowingly, reasonably sure he didn't actually have to say anything just yet, although this was for him uncharted participatory classroom territory. "And if I suggested to you that the Supreme Court has been drifting toward a decidedly more liberal acceptance of the reasonable regulation of business, what would be the significance of *Euclid v. Ambler Realty?*"

Huh?

"And a couple of Friday afternoon bonus points if you can answer these questions." She seemed to loosen up a bit. "First, can you tell me whether this drift is consistent with the Holmes-Brandeis philosophy of regulatory review?"

Bonus points? Holmes—what?

"And second."

What now?

"Can you tell me the name—and the release date—of the James Taylor album you have been dialed into for the last, oh, ten minutes?

How could she—

The students in the front turned toward the back, sensing something was about to pop. First-year law is like feeding time around the watering hole in the Serengeti—the weak and lame are doomed, and everybody knows it.

Even the folks over at Disney Studios don't hide this reality, even from the kids.

Thomas was not *wholly* unprepared, and not every sorry gazelle gets devoured on those Tanzanian grasslands, or in *Admin Law I* for that matter. Just the dumb ones. To be fair, he had read most of the materials the night before, but clearly not deeply. He had no idea who or what *Euclid* or *Ambler Realty* were, or why they had harnessed the machinery of the American legal system, only to begin a complicated journey ending up serving him up for an early Friday evening meal. But he was up on his James Taylor, and he had a fifty-fifty shot at the first bonus question, a simple *yes* or *no* gamble.

"Professor Olsen." *Go big, or go home.* "Yes, *Ambler Realty* is, without a doubt, *not* consistent with Holmes-Brandeis." Thomas paused, going big in the bonus round with a kind of Outward-Bound, ruggedly wholesome confidence softened with a bit of minor league charm.

"And I do apologize for drifting a bit to the sweet sounds of James Taylor's second album, *One Man Dog.*"

Don't push it.

"Released in October of 1972." Thomas pushed it.

There was a bit of nervous laughter up in the front rows, where, rumor had it, the smart students lived, true titans of the Serengeti.

"And as to your question-in-chief," Thomas liked the lawyerly sound of that, "the significance of *Ambler Realty* rests in its ability to clarify to the Court what the Court needed clarifying."

Clarifying to the Court what the Court needed clarifying?

Professor Maryellen Olsen carefully removed her glasses, took a soft cloth from the lectern, and began cleaning the lenses. She just looked so… *disappointed.* Fixing her gaze on the lame gazelle, her arm began a curious and expansive arc as she uttered words which would echo through Roberts Hall lore for generations:

"With answers like that, YOU WILL NEVER OWN YOUR OWN HOME."

Was that a—?

The professor put her glasses back on, perhaps better to see the idiot with the large moustache and no brain in the back row.

"*Class.*" She paused. "The regulation of business—once a suspect use of government powers—is now quite liberally tolerated by the Court, particularly since *Euclid v. Amber Realty Co.,* a case decided in 1926 which sustained comprehensive municipal zoning." She paused again. "Wholly *consistent* with the Holmes-Brandeis philosophy of limited judicial review."

Smart first-year law students never bet against the house.

Idiot first-year law students should not even enter the house, and if they do, just take a dive when outgunned. Thomas considered jumping out the window, but before he could make the move the professor added, "But nice try on James Taylor. It was actually *Mud Slide Slim and the Blue Horizon,* released in April of 1971." Assistant Professor Maryellen Olsen shrugged. "Not his best. See me after class, Mister Bickford."

—⁂—

Law school is not usually the place for wild rumor.

But within minutes word spread that the Serengeti had claimed another first-year law student, brought down by what quickly became known as "The Curse of Maryellen Olsen," soon to become simply "The Curse." And just as quickly nervous first-year law students began researching the possible distinction between a *curse* and a *spell*, and whether there were *jurisdictional limits* to either—the professor's wide arcing arm gesture a puzzling, but alarming, bit of performance art. Some argued it was *prima facie* simply a curse for Thomas to carry alone. The middle grounders claimed that it extended only to those actually in close proximity to Thomas Bickford's seat, or at worst just the classroom. At the more worrisome end, a few feared that it had been laid on the entire first-year class, and *in perpetuity*.

Thomas, for his part and with a certain nobility, tried for months to push the case that The Curse was his alone, a singular burden he pledged to carry with as much dignity as he could muster.

Other spectacular classroom humiliations would follow, of course, not all of which were Thomas Bickford's. These included the rare maiming of a third-year law in the notoriously treacherous *Conflict of Laws Section II* seminar, the public flogging of a sassy second-year law over in *Creditor's Rights I*, and the complete meltdown of a transfer student in *Domestic Relations* who had drifted down from some law school in Montana, much to her peril.

In due course talk of The Curse quieted down, and Thomas even took in stride the inevitable toast made to it at the class graduation party two years later. And each year thereafter at his law class reunions.

—※—

The Law is, indeed, a learned profession, although Thomas was not happy to learn that the law of curses and spells is thin indeed, and the remedies few, even under the quirky law of Louisiana and the municipal code of Savannah, Georgia. And in the end, the law treated Thomas Aquinas Bickford III quite well, and he returned the favor. He raised a family in homes that were loved, chasing the magic metrics of refinancing and the American siren call of the ever-larger home. Now retired—he likes to tell people he is fully recovered from the practice of law—he lives with his wife of forty-one years in a happy ramshackle of a home along the Georgia coast, Spanish Moss swinging lazily from the live oaks along the tidal high-water line. It is a good marriage, in a home filled with laughter.

And as they have for years now, they walk most evenings to the end of their crabbing dock, each with a glass of wine. There are just two chairs on the dock, and an old table.

It's their private place, and special, particularly on the first Friday of the month when Thomas tucks his checkbook into the deep pocket of his wrinkled khakis.

Thomas is of the old school, only recently migrating from his faithful flip-phone to a smart phone. And his wife—she of smarter stuff—brings an iPod playlist. And like clockwork, Maryellen Olsen Bickford hugs her husband, the sounds of James Taylor drifting over the quiet marsh. She whispers in his ear, not for the first time, how she was just messing with him that day in *Admin Law I* so many years ago.

He then writes another check to Sun Coast Mortgage, and they both smile.

Fifty Cents
on the Dollar

The trunk was the old leather kind, a scuffed black with rusty brass fittings. Its lock was nothing more than a suggestion, a curious set of stenciled block numbers fading away on the top left corner of the lid.

C. B. "Bunny" deBose had mostly forgotten about it, lost as it was in the deeper shadows of the attic of his mother's home. The socket in the single hanging attic fixture had long ago gone bad, and the tiny peaked window set high on the western side of the house welcomed the sunlight's skittish dance across the floor for only the briefest of moments, especially in the winter. Like most old homes along the tidal marsh the attic was filled with the stuff of generations, and as a boy he would help his mother carry things up its narrow steps, which had a tight midpoint landing.

He didn't like it up there, but for reasons that seemed to change over the years. At first it was the thatch of sticky cobwebs that entangled the boxes and trunks and old pieces of furniture, cobwebs which seemed to be thickest at the top of the stairs and in the darkest corners. His mother would gently pull them out of his hair, reminding him that the cobwebs were a *good thing*, there to anchor the stuff of lives and memories and lore so that it all not simply float away.

"All ours," she would say, *"the things that ground us."*

When he was older, she would point to what seemed to be the most ordinary of stuff up in that attic, although to her—and he could sense this even as a young boy—they were anything but. There was the old captain's chair, and she would ask him to imagine his grandfather listening to the burdens of a small tenant farmer in the Great Depression as he sat in that chair in the small law office on the second floor of the old bank building, on Lawyers' Row. Next to it was the apothecary from a now-shuttered candy store in town, and she would ask him to remember the smile on a child's face when his aunt, who lost the store half a century ago, threw in an extra candy bar for free. And on the floor was the glass case housing a hand-rigged model of an old three-masted schooner, and she would ask him to think of the pain of the disgraced banker from New Orleans forced to sell it at auction, the banker's tether to their family twice-removed but close enough to share the shame. Each *thing* seemed to talk to her, stories of the good and the bad absorbed into the aged wood and cardboard boxes and glass cases and all the rest. "The stuff of *life*," she would say, "the ordinary of love and loss, mischief and folly, and everything in-between."

But not, she would add, ordinary to everyone.

And once, as the pocked lower branches of a live oak brushed against the home's tin roof, she gently touched his shoulder. In a soft whisper she asked him to take a good look around the room, then close his eyes and listen to what it all was saying.

Only years later, when he returned to his boyhood home to do what Carter Elizabeth Moraine had asked him to do, would he, too, finally understand.

—⁓—

Bunny deBose grew up in the old Victorian near Goose Creek Crossing, South Carolina, a place that had been in the family for nearly a century, unencumbered by either debt or trespass. He was an only child and popular with his classmates. Of modest abilities but diligent and quick with a smile, Bunny earned a partial academic scholarship to Southern Wesleyan, a small Christian college not far from home. He seemed to be doing conventionally well when in the late spring of

1967, in his third year, he decided—and quite on impulse, as it was an impulsive time—to join a free-spirited Wofford art major on some cross-country, drop-out, *summer-to-who-knows-when* adventure in a dusty lime-green VW van. The van's name was *Lucy*—painted in a careful red script across a small patch of blue sky, with puffy white clouds and small diamonds, under the driver's side window—and her name was Carter Elizabeth Moraine.

She and Bunny had grown up together—or at least *sideways*, as children do in small towns everywhere—casually aware of one another since she moved to Goose Creek Crossing from somewhere near Baltimore. She was in her sixth grade; Bunny in his fifth.

It was all so very Sixties—vague, self-absorbed, a confused blend of hope and adventure and resignation, and *important* in some unspoken way. They were youth of modest privilege on the cusp of things uncertain, not the least of which was Bunny's relationship with his local draft board. It had yet to be anything but cordial, and relatively unthreatening: he had not exactly *un-enrolled* from college, with its golden draft deferment which still attached, at least in theory. He had just *slipped away* from his studies, that detail more or less left hanging. He also figured that his draft board, even if they did catch on, would conclude that his left leg, shorter than his right after polio as a child, was not good soldier material.

Carter Elizabeth had no such pressing draft issues, other than hating the whole idea of the war. And *her* legs were in perfect harmony, long and tanned and something Bunny had paid little attention to until their casual friendship drifted into something more at the Crossing Christian Academy they both attended before college, where her father served as head of school and his mother briefly taught European History. They continued to date after graduation, things moving along in ragged fits and spurts. Bunny was vaguely aware of some other guy named Mason, who was either a real jerk or some kind of poet-genius somewhere up in Maryland, as well as a lacrosse player at Carolina, who mostly seemed to be a good guy but always injured.

So off they went—no more talk of Mason or the lacrosse guy—young love in the moldy VW bus, its floorboard patched with cardboard, the whole thing floating atop the frothy promise of those Aquarian days, as well as the four new tires her father had bought at the beginning of her senior year for his daughter's trips back and forth from college. The back bench seats were soon littered with the flotsam of things far removed from their earlier days: clothes-stuffed duffels, two sleeping bags, a smelly canvas tent bought at a surplus store, a soft cotton children's blanket decorated with three puffy bunny rabbits, cigarettes—for her, he didn't smoke—junk food, mainly Doritos, cheap wine, and a little grass for her, at least mostly.

Resting atop it all was a painted plaster figure of Mr. Albert Einstein. It was an utterly absurd thing, maybe a foot tall and hand painted by artisans in Taos, New Mexico. At least that's what they were told when they bought him on a rainy day for three dollars at a flea market near Asheville.

Mr. Einstein joined the fun fully assembled, his enormous mane of white cotton hair and his plaster-bushy white moustache wholly in character. His brow was noticeably furrowed, not surprising for a man burdened by the many strange things going on in the universe—any number of which could be troublesome—as well as the whole business of the atomic bomb, for which he was just a small contributing writer although people think he was much more.

He stood on a wide base that Carter Elizabeth said—and he remembers this so vividly—*would look so cool on their own mantelpiece someday.* And she soon discovered two things about their new companion. First, there was no "Hand Painted by Artisans in Taos" sticker on the base, something they didn't check before they bought him, and they quickly concluded he had likely come from some dingy operation in Jersey. And second, Mr. Einstein's long and bony-figured hands could pop right out of the sleeves of his coat, just above the wrist. In one of the pop-out hands he was holding a cigarette, and in the other he was flashing the *V*-sign for peace.

It wasn't quite artistic, but switching his hands around and twisting them in ways never imagined by some contract-plaster-artist in Hoboken was endlessly amusing, particularly for a Wofford art major when she had smoked a little weed. And once, when they passed a slow-moving convoy of olive-green Army half-trucks somewhere in North Carolina near Fort Bragg, Carter Elizabeth held Mr. Einstein out her passenger-side window and wiggled his peace hand. Soldiers in the back of the trucks *V*-flashed it back, with huge grins. But when Bunny sped up to pass the lead jeep, the driver flipped them off.

They both figured he was regular army, and let it go at that.

Not long after, one of Mr. Einstein's hands fell off and shattered. It was, at least at that moment, his left one, and the one holding the cigarette. Carter Elizabeth figured maybe the old boy was telling her something, and she vowed to stop smoking—a vow she broke some thirty-eight miles further down the road. They quickly agreed that they didn't want to risk losing his peace hand, stopping at a Quick Mart to buy some Elmer's glue and sticky electric tape to plug the gaping hole in his left sleeve. With care, they then glued the peace hand permanently into his right sleeve.

It was a strange time, indeed.

The lengthening shadow of Vietnam had made everyone a little crazy, the tired soul of the country up for grabs. Passions were raw and overheated, acts of political and social theater the bouncy ball of rebellion that many hopped aboard. Years later people would say that Vietnam was the first foreign war fought on American soil, and that, at least for Bunny deBose, finally put a lid on it.

But if the war had informed so many tangled personal choices during those years, the whole idea of his dropping out had more to do with the pull of Carter Elizabeth's liquid green eyes—he would always remember how they sparkled with mischief when she said they could at least *play hippies* for a while—the softness of her voice after a little wine, and her healthy interest in getting laid after a little more.

"*Cohm ohn,* Bunny," she teased him in an accent which from time to time seemed to pop out of nowhere, more Baltimore than Goose Creek Crossing. *"It's our Gypsy Summer!"*

And it was. At least for a while.

—⁊⁊⁊—

They traveled mostly the back roads of the South, finding odd jobs and a certain freedom in the chaos of the times. Their talks in the beginning were unhurried and deep, seeding a magic that they would have been forgiven to think was love in that summer of 1967. But as they rolled along towards a future both unhurried and uncertain, Bunny could sense a change—a tug backwards, a pull from something in her past, a shadow from some place dark or some secret closely held. It worked like a mirror, reflecting her back to some primary truths holding her—and them—back as she struggled to find new ones.

They were not alone on the back roads of the country that summer, other middle-class gypsies rolling along like lost marbles, and much of their adventure was shared.

This was not always a good thing.

When camping with others, Carter Elizabeth seemed all too willing to drift toward the darker corners of the times, and closer to the edgier counter-culture of serious drugs. As far as Bunny could tell, she was not fooling around with the really bad stuff, although one night, under a clear and moonlit canopy of stars, she tried some psylocibin. It terrified them both.

He would like to think that he had come close to breaking through to her. But he was no match for that mirror, or the drugs. Her essential loneliness worked like a slow poison, a dark river of sadness growing between them. One night—he remembers it as a campground in a tall forest of loblolly pines, probably in the Carolinas—she opened up about her brother, something she had never done before. She told him that he had gone missing somewhere over North Vietnam in the late spring, a young lieutenant flying an F-4 on a mission off the *Intrepid,* and that he had been scheduled to rotate home in less than a month.

And Bunny realized that night just what lay unspoken between them, and had been there all along—the cruel unfairness that he would likely avoid the draft, his uneven left leg granting him a reprieve, a chance pardon from the madness while so many others went off to war.

So on a warm late summer day, in the picture-perfect square of a small town in Tennessee, they sat down on a worn bench near the statue of a young soldier killed in another war which had torn the country apart, and she told him she needed to *go it alone,* at least for a now. She said she felt parts of herself—important parts—missing in her own life, and that she had to find them, by herself, before she could truly love another.

Bunny deBose and Carter Elizabeth Moraine then said goodbye. Their parting—as these things go—was surprisingly gentle, all wispy and soft like the better cuts of a Maryanne Faithful album, their tears of the gentler sort, like a morning mist. And as she held him, she whispered that someday, just maybe, they would laugh together about their gypsy summer days with Mr. Einstein.

And their last dollar bill.

How he remembered that last dollar bill.

"We'll tape it all back together, like we did Mr. Einstein." She paused. "Just like we'll put the pieces of this country back together, too. Someday, Bunny. You'll see."

Bunny wasn't so sure, about any of it. He sat for hours on that worn bench, hoping the lime green van would come back around.

"Cohm ohn, Bunny"—that's what he hoped she would say—*"you jump back ohn in."*

—⁊⁊—

That's the soft voice, with a sometimes Baltimore accent, that Bunny heard as he opened the trunk. In it was an old navy uniform, a moldy sleeping bag, and a single black and white portrait of Carter Elizabeth Moraine, with a torn dollar bill in the lower right corner.

You see, just a week before they parted those years ago she had charmed some kid working in a struggling photography studio in Nashville to cut them a deal on a slimmed-down portrait package, just three black and white photos, each a five by seven. In one they posed as a couple, smiling. The other two were individual portraits, taken against a simple curtained wall. There wouldn't be time or the cash for an album of proofs, or really any proofs at all: the best the kid could promise was to pick the best takes himself, the only way to get it done fast and at budget.

They splurged on a room at the Rest-A-Way Country Cottages, a sketchy motel just outside town so that they could scrub up for the shoot. They spent an hour at a funky consignment shop that after-noon, bargaining for what they called their *portrait clothes*, although just from the waist up. She found a simple dark blue sweater and pink blouse; he a blue oxford button down shirt which had been brought into the store freshly cleaned and starched. When they showered and dressed the next morning—her long blonde hair washed, and then washed again, Bunny's hair brushed back and neat—Carter Elizabeth added a simple gold cross on a chain, something Bunny had never seen her wear before. He joked that that it looked like they were back in Goose Creek Crossing and off to a Sunday picnic, and even the cranky old guy behind the check-out counter smiled as they handed in their keys, pleased that at least this couple seemed to be on the right path.

The shoot was quick, and the couple did indeed look more like young marrieds than mini-hippies, happy smiles all around.

Just before they left the studio, Carter Elizabeth turned to Bun-ny. With a sweet smile, she reached into her jeans back pocket. It was slightly torn with a sewn-on peace symbol, and she pulled out three bills: two twenties—that was the deal she cut with the kid, cash only, no receipt given or expected—and one single, each bill bank-teller fresh. She handed the twenties to the photographer, and then handed the single to Bunny.

"You just tear it in half, Bunny deBose." He now remembers her eyes that day—brighter than he had seen in weeks. "But gently. Very gently."

Bunny did just that. The tear was crisp and nearly straight. "Fine, Carter. Now what?"

"Now, *cohm ohn*, Bunny. You just hang in here with me for a minute more." She grinned, with a kind of *ta-da* hand-flourish. "The moment of truth. Now you hand me the two halves." Her eyes still twinkled.

"This some kind of magic trick?" Bunny was amused, but this was turning a little strange.

Carter Elizabeth shook her head, took the two pieces of the once-whole dollar bill from Bunny, then turned to the kid. He looked confused too, but seemed relieved that the two twenties had arrived in his hands intact. "Think you can fit these half-dollars under the glass in each of our framed portraits?" She handed the kid the two pieces. "The solo shots."

"Sure, why not?"

"Maybe just put each piece in a lower corner, don't you think?"

"Yeah, won't block anything that way." The kid thought for a moment. "You got anything you want under the glass in the third frame?" He did not seem to be kidding.

Carter Elizabeth laughed, but not unkindly. "That's it, man. We're just a couple travelin' hippies outa bread. That's our last dollar."

—⁂—

The portraits were good, each half-of-the-dollar bill nicely positioned on the lower right corner of the two solo shots, just as Carter Elizabeth had asked. She handed Bunny her portrait, and he handed his to her.

"Not too bad for a forty-buck investment." Bunny smiled.

"You mean not bad for a forty-one dollar investment."

"Well, it's just fifty cents on that last dollar, Carter, for both of us."

They laughed, and asked the kid to wrap the frames carefully for their travels. Bunny packed his away in his duffel bag, and Carter did the same in hers. They decided to tape the picture of them together to the back of the seat, like a city cabbie.

—∭—

Bunny hung around that small town in Tennessee for a few weeks, working odd jobs in a kind of fog before hitching his way back home to Goose Creek Crossing with just his duffel bag, memories, and her picture. Carter Elizabeth kept Mr. Einstein, the portrait taped to the seat, and a large piece of Bunny deBose's heart.

He did not return to college, at least just yet. Instead, he borrowed a car and drove to the Navy base in Charleston and asked the young Marine corporal at the gate where a young man could join up. This was not the usual way of things, but it all got sorted out when a young officer showed up and directed him to a recruiting station downtown.

There was a little flap about his short left leg, but he eventually got his waiver and passed the physical, some wiseass corpsman writing on his forms that he should be assigned to a ship which lists to starboard, just to even things out. But he tested out well, especially in auditory proficiency, and spent the next three years listening for Russian submarines in the North Atlantic on a tired destroyer which did, indeed, list to starboard.

His war was the cold one, and over quickly. When he got out he went back to school, getting his degree in history. He did not hear from Carter Elizabeth when he was in the service, although he suspected she may have heard he joined up. At least he hoped she had.

After graduating, Bunny moved to Atlanta to take a teaching job at a small private school near Buckhead. There he met, and soon married, a young woman he met on a blind date, but that tanked in the sixth season. Bunny was rattling around when not long after his divorce he received a package from a Mr. Charles T. Moraine, of 2342 Lansdowne Rd, Goose Creek Crossing, South Carolina.

It wasn't a large package, just over a foot tall, but heavy.

He opened it, and found Mr. Einstein. The genius was a little worse for wear, but his left hand was still taped and the *V*-peace hand still glued in place. There was also a note on the crisp cream stationery of the Crossing Christian Academy:

> *Dear Bunny,*
>
> *I am sending this to what our alumni records show is your correct address, although I reluctantly trespass with the sad news of Carter Elizabeth's death last spring. I have enclosed a clipping of her obituary, which does justice neither to her life nor the tragedy of her death. There are so many unanswered questions, but for now I will carry those burdens privately. But I do know that she talked often of her one great adventure, her "gypsy summer" with you. She also left a note, and her mother and I will carry those burdens privately and we will guard her confidences fiercely. And that is as it should be. I make, however, this exception: she specifically asked that we return Mr. Albert Einstein to you, and I am honoring that request.*
>
> *In sadness,*
> *Charles Moraine*

Bunny didn't read the clipping, at least that day. He didn't need to. But as he picked up the plaster figure he noticed something scratched into the base. It was fine but deep, like the cut of a sculptor's knife, where he knew for sure nothing had been before.

It said simply: *Remove the tape.*

It wasn't hard to do, at least physically, and inside the hollow arm was a rolled paper, pink and smooth. He fished it out, and as he unrolled it the torn half of a dollar bill fell out. He began to read the graceful script of an artist's hand:

> My dear Bunny,
>   Under maybe a billion stars along a lake somewhere in the Carolinas, that magic and frightening and wonderful gypsy summer we spent together, you said this to me: that we were like swimmers caught in a rip tide, our best chance of survival simply to swim parallel to the shore until we could safely head back. Oh, dear Bunny, you made it back, and I didn't. But you know that now, and I pray that you will never know all the details, or go looking for them. And, as you can see, I'm counting on you still having that other half of our last dollar, and my portrait too. I don't think I told you it was the only portrait I ever liked. Perhaps, even under the circumstances, you will see your way to sliding my half dollar under the frame, next to yours.
>   You were always the one, Bunny deBose.
>
>   Love always,
>   Carter Elizabeth

On the back of the note were puffy white clouds on a blue sky, with small yellow diamonds inside. They were drawn precisely with artists' pencils, the blue just as he remembered from his gypsy summer.

—m—

Carter Elizabeth was right, of course. Bunny knew exactly where he had put her portrait, wrapped in newspaper and tucked under his old Navy uniform in his service trunk. He had lugged the trunk up to the attic of his mother's home years earlier, wheeling it around that awkward mid-point landing and then shoving it into a corner.

On a crisp fall afternoon a week after Mr. Moraine's package arrived, Bunny took Carter Elizabeth's note, along with the half-dollar and Mr. Einstein, up to that attic. He gently peeled the newspaper wrapping from her picture—he noticed it was a back page from the Charleston *Post and Courier*—and did exactly what she had suggested, tucking her half bill into a corner of the frame, just touching the one already waiting there. He stood over the open trunk, holding the portrait in his trembling hand and not wanting to do anything. In a moment, he sat down in his grandfather's captain's chair, and looked around.

The stuff of life. Listen to their voices.

Bunny deBose closed his eyes, and did just that, just *listened*—to a gentle rustle of the wind outside, the scratching of that tired branch against the tin roof, the sounds of some young boys playing outside. And then—in something less than even a whisper—he heard it:

"Cohm ohn, Bunny. It's where I want to be."

He took a last look at the portrait—he would for years talk about how intense a simple black and white portrait can be, mostly in the eyes, but never with any specifics. He then placed it back in to the trunk.

The stuff of love and loss, and everything in-between.

He next took Carter Elizabeth's hand-written note, rolled it up, and placed it back in Mr. Einstein's hollow left arm, carefully sealing him up with some electrical tape just as he had done years ago. He turned the old genius upside down and began to scrape away Carter Elizabeth's instructions until there was but a hint of something mysterious, something that would remain very private.

He thought she would like that.

Bunny tidied things up, then closed the lid. He took Mr. Einstein home with him and carefully placed him on a mantle, just as Carter Elizabeth had said they would, someday.

But he did it alone.

Casual Friday

"It's a wonderful thing, and been around a long time, you know."

The Honorable Sydney M. Kaplan, Senior Judge for the Twelfth Judicial Circuit, waved a robed arm towards Courtroom 3B just beyond the closed door to his chambers. "When *credible*, it seems to move things right along. We call it *evidence,* and it pops up all the time around here." The judge paused, glaring at the two young attorneys. "But I've been waiting to see something like it all morning." He then nodded to the court reporter who had followed them in to chambers. "We're off the record here."

Tony d'Mazzio, just six months out of Brooklyn Law and seven weeks into his job as Assistant Public Defender, wasn't sure if that was by the book. Meredith Rankin, Assistant District Attorney, didn't care: the whole morning had been a disaster, swallowed up by the APD's unexpected motion to suppress a defendant's statement, a short but damning handwritten thing which was her whole case. If that was not enough, the rumpled reporter sitting in the back of the courtroom was already smelling a story—even though the docket in 3B today should have been a real *nothing,* mostly pre-trial motions and pleas in cases of minor trespass against the good order of the city.

The chambers were cramped, and hot. Before sitting down the judge loosened his tie, started to unzip his black robe, then stopped. Had it been other than a summer Friday morning he would likely have unzipped to a full judicial disrobe. But the crusty judge had recently taken to ditching even a blazer on Casual Fridays, as well as wearing short sleeved, drip-dry, tangerine- or lemon-colored shirts, khaki pants, and scuffed Topsiders *without socks*. He topped-off with the occasional long-billed fisherman's cap and a wide-bodied lime-green, 1940's *movie-stupid* tie. His wife Barbara, herself a lawyer, bought the tie for the judge at a vintage clothing store as a gag gift, mostly because of the dozens of gold-hued images of the *Scales of Justice* printed on it. And if you looked closely, one sly eye was peeking out from behind each of their blindfolds.

She had never expected him to actually *wear* the tie, of course.

Indeed, the judge enjoyed his reputation as old-school. For years, on a strict daily rotation he had worn to work one of five midnight-blue, three-button worsted wool suits, classically matched with white long-sleeved and heavily starched batiste cotton spread-collar shirts, hand-sewn Italian club ties, braces (but only in the genuine English style, buttoned to the waistband), and black Cole-Hahn closed-lace half-brogues.

And socks, of course, always calf-length and black.

But much to the sly delight of his wife, the judge began wearing the gag tie to work on summer Casual Fridays. As sartorial—or even judicial—rebellions go, it was mild. But the judge, a careful guardian of whatever dignity still attached to his thankless job in the criminal court, did his best to keep his Lady Justice tie, along with its Casual Friday supporting cast, a quiet trespass. Now, each Friday he would remember to keep his black robes fully zipped up to the brim, allowing just a peek of *something lime going on under there* but nothing too disturbing to the good order of his court.

None of this was much on his mind as the judge rounded his cluttered wooden desk. The tall-backed leather chair squeaked as he sat down, the two lawyers remaining standing. A small fan, perched atop a stack of papers in the corner of the chambers, bobbed from side to side, its rhythmic rotations making an annoying metallic noise at each turn. Atop a stand-alone bookcase under a large and gracefully curved window was an *actual* Scales of Justice, a well-polished brass beauty standing almost two feet tall. A ceramic coffee mug on each carriage arm—*Seton Hall* on the left, *The World's Greatest Grampa* on the right—kept the scales in perfect balance.

And this Lady's blindfold was centered, and tight. Justice—at least in this corner of the world—was blind.

—ɯ—

"You two have been dancing around all morning." He turned to the public defender. "You're on thin ice, Mr. d'Mazzio." The judge then looked over to the ADA. "You, too, Ms. Rankin." He paused, waiting for one more click of the fan rounding the corner. "But I haven't figured out just why yet. But it's a circus out there." He turned to the court reporter, looking for a sympathetic nod. "And that reporter—what's his name, Jankey? Starts with a J—half asleep as usual, until you two started in on it."

The two lawyers knew none of this invited a response, at least not yet. They also knew that the judge ran a tight, but fair, courtroom, and that he had worked his way up through the system the hard way—night law school while a beat cop in the city. That was followed by stints as both a public defender and an assistant DA before taking a high-profile partnership at Simpson & Ballentine, where he made both his bones and reputation. This was all rewarded with a seat on the bench some twenty years ago, and a vested retirement in three weeks.

But neither knew anything for certain about the Lady Justice tie, although there had been quiet talk for a few months among the clerks that the usual starched Judge Kaplan was wearing *some pretty crazy stuff* on Fridays during the summer. Both the ADA and the APD had hoped—they confessed this over a drink a few weeks later—for a little more zipper and a confirming glance to offer clear evidence to support a good bench story, the kind young lawyers love over a few beers.

The judge turned to the APD.

"Mr. d'Mazzio, I've given you plenty of room this morning. But you've got to give me something. *Anything...*" The judge paused. "But a bunny rabbit?" He looked tired. "A six-foot-four *pink* bunny rabbit. That's what you got?"

"Your Honor, as I started to say—"

"Yeah. The kid signs the statement because... because *a bunny rabbit made him do it?*" The judge shook his head, paused, then turned to the assistant district attorney. She was just two years into the job. "Jump in anytime, Ms. Rankin."

She smoothed the sleeve of her blouse, which only added to her crisp, all-business demeanor. She was polished and pedigreed—Wellesley, Notes Editor on the *Law Review* at Virginia. Word was going around that she was getting ready to take a strong six-figure partnership-track position in the white-collar firm of Kaufman, Stafford & McNulty at its tony office just three blocks away. She could see its gleaming glass as she glanced, but just for a second, out the large window.

"The statement is sound, Your Honor. Signed, handwritten, all by the book." She hesitated. "I can bring in Detectives Alvarez and Dewberry if we continue over to next week." She paused. "Counsel can cross all morning, Your Honor, but you'll find no six-foot—"

"Six-foot-four, Meredith." The APD had been explicit about that all morning.

"Okay. No six-foot-*four* pink bunny rabbit, hopping around the Third Precinct when they are questioning—"

"*Interrogating*, Your Honor." D'Mazzio played his money card. "The kid's—"

"*Not even under arrest at that point.*" The ADA played hers. "No custodial restraint. He could have walked."

"So why does he cough up that nifty statement? Well, I'll tell you why, Your Honor." Tony d'Mazzio was on a roll. "I hear that clown Mahoney down at the Third Precinct, well, he's been finding ways to mess with these street kids for years. Good cop, pretty good cop, bad cop. Why not just throw in a *bunny* cop? So here's how it goes down. Mahoney rents the bunny costume on a dare—it's like a size 55 Extra Tall, they got a couple, *a couple,* can you believe it?—over at that novelty shop uptown. I checked. Anyway, he talks Alvarez and Dewberry into having a little fun. They bring the kid in, but best I can tell nobody really thinks he's really done *anything,* just one of those kids in the hood they figure is up to *something,* everyone just fishing around. But they know it will be busy at the station, Friday night and all, and soon it all begins to fall in place: all three interrogation rooms are full, so Alvarez and Dewberry suggest to the kid they just go for a *chat* in a small office on the second floor. They buy the kid a coke, talk a little sports trash, complain about the weather. No tapes running—the room not even equipped, real quiet. Then—the kid's ready to testify to this, Your Honor—Alverez and Dewberry take a break. *Just for a minute,* they say. The kid doesn't know he can walk, Your Honor—"

"He's right about walking, Your Honor, it was non-custodial."

"—and next thing he knows this *thing* pops into the room, all pink and moldy-cotton smelly, all *six foot four.* The kid's *terrified.* The bunny rabbit starts bouncing around like some looney, *squealing* the kid tells me, pink cotton hands the size of a catcher's mitt flailing about. *I* would have been terrified." He paused. "Mahoney—it had to be Mahoney, Your Honor—didn't need to lay a hand on him."

The fan took another metallic turn as the APD hesitated.

"*Squealing,* Ms. District Attorney. That Mahoney's so dumb he can't remember if he's playing Elmer Fudd or Bugs himself." He paused. "The kid would've signed anything to get that crazy man to leave." He paused again. "Your Honor, my client's been clean for less than a month, probably thought he was going drug-crazy too. Told me he was lucky he didn't poop in his—"

"Got the picture, counselor." The judge turned to the assistant DA. "Jump in anytime, Ms. Rankin."

"Simply didn't happen that way. Pure fantasy. The kid coughed it up all on his own, the tape clean."

"Yeah." d'Mazzio injected. "The tape when they finally get into a *real* interrogation room—"

"No bunnies pulling detective pay around here, Your Honor. The statement is admissible."

"No way." The APD pushed it. "You know the crap's been going down over at the Third, Meredith."

"ADMISSIBLE, Your Honor." The ADA pushed back. "Respectfully, let's move this thing along."

The judge held up both hands, looked out his window, then turned to the two lawyers. "Let me ask you both something. You remember your algebra?"

Both lawyers nodded, although not convincingly.

"Well, here's how I remember it. Multiply a negative by a negative and you get a positive." The judge shrugged. "My court, day after day— going on twenty years now—is just like that. *Algebra.* I take two negatives—the bullshit and the half-truths that seep into the game from both sides—and then I multiply them to get something close to a result I—we—can live with."

The judge waved his arms high in a circle, with a little flourish towards the window and the city outside. "No, maybe it's not your blind justice." The judge pointed toward the scales on the book case. "And I guess I kind of peek through that blindfold. But it's the best I can do."

He rose and straightened his tie. "Ms. Rankin, the statement's out, and without the statement you're high and dry." The judge zippered his robe just a notch, up to the brim. "This is a nothing case, Ms. Rankin. Receiving stolen goods? Give me a break. Enough stolen crap around that neighborhood to stock a Walmart. Whole case never should've been brought. Or, at worst, pleaded out—supervised probation, the kid's record open to a clean swipe in a year."

The judge looked at the APD. "When we go back out, I will entertain your motion to suppress, Mr. d'Mazzio."

The judge looked at the ADA. "You can object, Ms. Rankin. But I will grant the motion. Without it, you're done. Fruit of the poisoned tree."

He turned back to the APD. "Mr. d'Mazzio, I expect you will then want to move to dismiss the charge, and I will grant that too." He paused.

"And here's the thing. This is the second time this month I've heard something about a pink bunny rabbit—a very *tall* pink bunny rabbit. Overheard another judge at lunch just the other day, and now this."

The judge paused, trying to remember the last time Detective Mahoney had testified in his court. *Two months ago? Three? Yeah, that was him in that mess of an aggravated assault trial. All six-foot-four of him.*

The judge glared at the assistant district attorney. "This funny-bunny shit *will* stop, Ms. Rankin. Clean it up before you move over to that shiny office up the street, and before that reporter finds his story. And Mr. d'Mazzio, you win this one." The judge frowned. "But you'll be back before this court with that kid all too soon, that's my guess. Let's just hope it's not before I take off these robes for good."

The judge looked out the window. *That's the real math around here,* he thought.

—⚏—

Judge Kaplan went home early that afternoon, his docket cleared for the day. He had again done his judicial algebra—*pretty fairly this time,* he thought, earning a two-finger scotch, Dewar's on-the-rocks. He folded himself into his wicker lounger on a brick patio, where he was soon joined by his wife of thirty-four years. She sat facing him on a small bench, a stack of glossy travel brochures at her side, cruises mostly.

"Good day?" She asked, although a bit absently in the way of such marital pleasantries.

The judge lifted his drink, then noticed that a bug had landed on his Friday tie, which he had taken off and carefully set on the small table to his side. Leaning over, he saw that his visitor was a brightly-speckled lady bug, and it was sitting dead center on the peeking eye of one of the tie's Scales of Justice.

"Casual Friday, you know." The judge turned to his wife, and smiled. "Yeah, all things considered, it was a good day."

McAllister's Asterisk

N ot long ago I stumbled upon Poquamscutt Harbor, a wrong turn off the interstate in Rhode Island and a growling stomach conspiring to land me for lunch at the Masked Mussel, a haphazard but inviting place on weathered pilings along the Narragansett Bay.

It's nothing fancy: a small bar with four stools and a dozen tables on the inside with a couple high-tops on the back deck, and the whole thing seemed to sway as nervously as the old boats tied along the dock. The tables inside were covered in red-and-white checkered tablecloths, changed fresh at least every other day. At least that's my guess.

I took a table inside and ordered a Bud Light on draft. An older man sitting at the bar turned around, grinned, and shook his head.

"Only beer anyone should drink around here's the local IPA." He paused. "A Captain's Daughter, but only in a chilled can."

I took his beer tip—glad I did—and we got to talking. "Well, how about another tip for lunch?"

"Easy one. The mussels with chorizo and tomatoes over toast, drizzled with garlic. House favorite."

Both tips were on the mark, and he seemed a friendly sort, so I asked him if would care to join me at my table. It had been a long drive for me, and I was ready for some light conversation. I call myself a freelance writer—at least that's the way I spin things after I lost my job at a small weekly in Providence—and you never know what stories might grow in a quiet corner of a place like the Masked Mussel.

"I think I'll do that."

He introduced himself as Joseph Caravaggio, and he quickly added that his friends all call him Joey. He was a talkative sort, and I let him carry the conversation as I mopped up that rich tomato sauce with some extra bread, the garlic a bit strong but, as the locals say, a wicked pleasure. He told me he had worked the lobster boats for over forty years—a tough but good life, he added, but not for a family man. He did not elaborate, and I sensed the shadows of a very different journey had things broken a few degrees either way long ago. He didn't, however, seem unhappy.

Or maybe he just hid it well as we all do when we tumble into our own gallery of *might-have-beens.*

He was also proving himself an enjoyable lunch companion, describing an old trawler he was restoring over in Newport, a friendship with a widow warming over in Warwick, and his annual trip to Cleveland to catch a baseball game. *But no night games,* he added, *and never a seat in the bleachers.*

That was a curious footnote, and I took the bait.

"You got something against night games and bleacher seats, Joey?" I resisted asking him why Cleveland.

He shrugged. "Not until we played a night game right here in town, last game of the season it was, back when we still had a baseball team." He paused. "*The Chowda Bowls.* Screwiest team you ever saw." His eyes seemed to lose focus, his words trailing off. "*Been a long time now, but I was there,*" he said to me, "*and I heard them…*"

But that all comes at the end of the story Joey Caravaggio told me that afternoon, and I let him wander around it slowly, as old men do. He took it back to the beginning, to the day almost twenty years ago when a ballplayer named McAllister drove into town, looking for a befuddled manager named T. D. Weldon, Jr.

—⏑—

Boyden Tinkerson McAllister eased his old car into a parking space along the left-field fence of the old wooden stadium, the lot empty except for one other car sitting under a faded sign, *Reserved for Manager*.

Under that, in smaller letters, it read *T. D. Weldon Jr.*

The comma was missing, and the dusty Ford Bronco parked there had a flat rear tire. McAllister would always remember those details about that first day in Poquamscutt Harbor, a town then well-served by a four-car ferry and less-well-served by a minor league baseball team in the Mid-Coastal Division of the Class A Patriot League.

His car—years earlier it had been a gleaming tomato-red 1992 Mercedes 560SL Roadster, now mottled like a standing bowl of to-mato bisque—was at least three sizes too small for McAllister's six-one, 297-pound frame. The passenger seat was littered with plastic cups and straws, crinkled bags of kettle-cooked potato chips, Big-Mac wrappers, an empty tin of Planter's Spanish Redskin Peanuts, and a half-eaten A&W foot-long chili-cheese dog. A loose blob of chili had burrowed into the car's center console, and the whole mess looked like those garbage patches floating around the mid-Pacific Ocean. McAl-lister had always liked to drive the back roads—nothing, he thought, beats a chicken-fried steak dressed with a loaded baked potato at a roadside place early in the evening, or a three-egg omelet with a dou-ble stack of home-made griddle cakes to begin the day's drive—and he had missed a turn earlier that morning, ending up in Bellows Corner, Massachusetts. *Such a curious town,* he thought, *and now I'm gonna be late getting to Poquamscutt Harbor.*

"You're late, McAllister. Get your sorry ass in here, now."

The voice was deep and all-Yankee, coming from the open window above the Ford, followed by a hand motioning to a side entrance to the old stadium's clubhouse.

—m—

McAllister entered a dark area under the stands, ducked under a low beam, and entered the office of the manager of the Poquamscutt Harbor Chowda Bowls Professional Baseball Club, Inc. The door had been left open, and he could hear a toilet flush behind another door in the back of the office, and then a gruff "Take a seat."

To McAllister's ear—an ear more attuned to the gentle country ways of Logan's Bluff, Georgia, than the lobster-snap of things Rhode Island—it sounded less a courtesy than a command.

A small chair that looked like it had come over with the Pilgrims sat facing the manager's desk. He lowered himself into it with a groan—the chair returned the favor—and looked around. The office, like most he had seen in his years of playing ball in the minor leagues, was spare and smelled like damp mulch. The manager's desk was surprisingly well-mannered, with just a few loose papers adrift. A slightly tarnished brass name plate sat at the near edge of the desk, and this time whoever made the thing had put the comma where it was needed: T. D. Weldon, Jr.

"But most everyone calls me *Starchy*."

A short man—late fifties, wearing a faded teal-green Chowda Bowls cap, matching sweatshirt with a large bleach stain, wrinkled khakis, scuffed topsiders, and a worried look—popped out of the lou. "Guess it's because I dress so *crisply*."

"Pleased to meet you, Starchy." Pudge tried to stand up, but was stuck.

"Uh, that *everyone* I mentioned? It don't include the boys come to play ball for me. They call me *Skipper*. I like that." He looked out the window. "Makes me feel like I'm running a real team here."

He settled in behind his desk, took off his hat, and stared at the enormous ballplayer stuffed into the now-sagging Pilgrim chair. "You eat your way up here Pudge?"

Ouch.

Starchy grunted, put on a pair of wire-rimmed glasses, shuffled those few papers on the corner of his desk, and then placed three sheets of paper, typed and legal-sized, in the center. The day was warm for early June in Rhode Island, a slight but welcomed breeze sneaking in from the open window. With it was a salty hint of the Bay, although like many boys growing up around the Georgia coast it was the pungent punch of the stuff coming over from the paper mills which would always have a curious pull for McAllister, something about a sense of place.

"So here's the deal." Starchy Weldon wasted few words. "We haven't gotten near a pennant in years, and I hear the League's about ready to pull the plug on the franchise. The owner's up to his elbows in debt, and I'm not far behind. Two weeks ago our back-up catcher winked at the bat boy, grabbed his mitt, said to no one in particular that he was *done,* then ducked into the clubhouse in the middle of the fourth inning of our night game in Pawtucket. *In the middle of the inning.*" He shook his head. "No one has seen him since. Five nights ago, this clown who claims to be our shortstop—name's Ham Grendelkin, runs around telling everyone he's over two yards and six inches tall, but fails to add that he is currently leading the league in wild throws to first—tells me in the top of the third at a home game that the kid who tosses free hot dogs into the stands is a no-show. Then he starts bellyaching that he's been counting on the flying dogs for his one hot meal of the day."

McAllister nodded, although his sympathies were beginning to run with this Grendelkin, hot dogs his idea of the perfect food too.

"And," the manager was on a roll, "we haven't seen the hot dog pilot since then either." Starchy found his bald spot, just left of center on his curiously over-sized head, and it seemed to grow as he rubbed it. "Front office forgot to pay him." He shook his head again, something Pudge McAllister noticed Starchy was also inclined to do. "Only had nineteen fans in the stands anyway." He sighed. "Bottom line? I'm on the griddle, and you... *just look at yourself, son.*" Starchy looked out the window, then back. "Was it that thing in, ah...Greensboro?"

"Greenville."

"Well, you know the whispers." Starchy, like any good parent, a suspicious spouse, or a minor league baseball manager simply trying to hold on, already knew the answer. But he also knew he had to ask. "*What happened?*"

—⁂—

What happened, almost four years ago to the day McAllister rode into Poquamscutt Harbor, was this:

The Greenville Granny Sox, atop the Highlands Division of the Double-AA Southern League, were hosting the Birmingham Blisters. The Sox first baseman was a fit 181 pounds of pure baseball promise, a twenty-four-year-old player popular around South Georgia where he was known as *Tink,* his boyhood nickname. On that humid night he was holding onto a .326 batting average, along with a nine-game hitting streak, most of his hair, and a frisky hazel-eyed graduate of the Savannah School of Cosmetology who was worried that he was using the wrong conditioner.

Tink McAllister had singled in the second inning, walked in the fifth, and was facing a 2-1 count at the plate in the eighth when he took unkindly to a brush-back thrown high and tight by the kid pitcher for the Blisters, a rookie just out of Fordham named Darryl Zinkke, although Zinkke insisted his name be pronounced *Shaw*. No one knew why, or ever asked.

Tink McAllister charged the mound, tackling the pitcher. Zinkke ended-up on top, McAllister pinned under with two cracked ribs and a sprained shoulder. He would learn of the serious disk damage to his back only hours later.

A thirty-day suspension from the League Commissioner followed, along with a botched back surgery and a slow, painful, and erratic recovery. Laid-up for months, he soon lost his way in a haze of pain pills and self-pity, double cheeseburgers with extra fries, and the booze. What finally washed ashore was no longer Tink McAllister but a beached whale of a man with a new nickname, courtesy of a second-rate sports reporter for the Greenville *Post-Guardian* named Elmers Daubert.

"Like the glue," Elmers would tell people, "but without the apostrophe."

Writing a stinging back page story months later, Elmers Daubert threw McAllister under the bus, calling him "a bloated disgrace who can no longer even bend down to tie his shoes. And," he added without mercy, "our very own *'Pudge'* McAllister can't even *bend up.*"

The story broke McAllister, the nickname stuck, and the now-Pudge was let go at the end of the season.

His cosmetologist decamped soon after, running off with the last of a joint savings account and an annoyingly thin older man who was selling time-shares in Myrtle Beach. Over the next few months friends would see a hint of the old Tink McAllister when he would yak on rookie pitchers and asshole reporters named Elmers. *Who names someone that anyway?* he would ask, then launch into reed-thin time-share salesmen who pop the collars on their pastel polo shirts and make more money on a single sale than he ever made in a full year playing ball.

But all that he kept from Starchy. "I drifted pretty far from shore, in a shitstorm I made for myself. That's what happened." Boyden Tinkerson McAllister looked hard at Starchy. "But I also came back."

—∞—

And then what happened is this:

Pudge eventually began selling time-shares himself, along the coast near Atlantic Beach, North Carolina. With this cruel irony not lost to him, his wobbly journey back after *that thing* in Greenville started with the job. He was in no way fully repaired, and he would never be: the days of even trying to tie his shoes, just as Elmers Daubert had said, were simply *over.* But with some help—he was always guarded about this—he managed to shake the pills, most of the booze, and a few of the regrets.

The cheeseburgers and double fries were a different story.

After a couple years selling those time-shares, he had cobbled together something of a life when he read that the Wilmington Wildcats were looking for a batting coach. The team was only semi-pro, loaded with almost-done players from the bargain basement minors. McAllister contacted them, and over a lunch at a fish house along the intracoastal—remarkably, he held the line at a shrimp salad and an unsweetened ice tea, even sending the bread back—he told them his story.

Everyone knows the salt air along the coastal Carolinas can work a little magic, and the Wildcats took him on.

At the beginning of his second year—on the team as well as sober—they agreed to add a little pinch-hitting to his duties. Pudge McAllister was soon launching towering pinch-hit homers that landed somewhere off the continental shelf, with fans quick to forgive the extra baggage he brought to the plate and his general inability to beat a snail to first base. The word spread swiftly through the minor league teams down South, and eventually North to Poquamscutt Harbor, that *there might be something left in McAllister yet.*

Even if he can't bend down to tie his shoes.

—⚉—

And that's how the breaks of the game brought Pudge McAllister and Starchy Weldon to this moment in the manager's office of the Poquamscutt Harbor Chowda Bowls, an office which smelled like damp mulch.

"Well, Pudge, I got this... *thing* sitting right here." Starchy looked at the typed and legal-sized paper sitting on his desk like it was coiled to strike. "Never seen nothin' like it, and I've been around. And that owner I mentioned? Well, he's some kind of boy-genius software guy up there in Boston with a fancy marketing degree from Babson, and he's telling me that this…" Starchy looked like was about to gag, "this… this *narrative* will sell. That's exactly what he said. '*This narrative will sell.*' I have no idea what he's talking about."

Pudge McAllister was wondering that too.

Starchy picked up the paper from his desk and waved it around in the air. "We are offering you," Starchy looked like he wanted to spray the paper with Lysol, "this… *no-ground-ball contract to play first base for the Poquamscutt Harbor Chowda Bowls Professional Baseball Club.* Sweet Jesus."

This what?

"*This what?* Yeah, that's what you're probably thinking. Me too. But this no-ground-ball-contract is all part of the *narrative,* you see, the strapping country kid from nowhere Alabama—"

"Georgia."

"—all promise and charm, then one night crashes and burns big time in Greensboro—"

"Greenville."

"—popping painkillers like vitamin D tablets. Loses the girl, the money, his way. Then he gains maybe 400 pounds sitting around eating double cheeseburgers and foot-long chili-cheese dogs and watching re-runs of *The Andy Griffith Show* on an Aaron Rent-to-Own big-screen Sony, hoping the rent's been paid. But somewhere along the dark side he gets help, crawls out of the bottle by selling time-shares. '*Time shares in Myrtle Beach, can you beat it?*' That's what the snotty boy-genius owner says." Starchy shook his head.

Pudge just shrugged.

"Anyway, next thing anyone knows the fallen hero has sobered up with some semi-pro team down on the coast, and he's launching pinch hit home runs somewhere out into the Bermuda Triangle." Starchy broke another almost-smile. "The boy-genius says, '*Who cares if he still can't tie his shoes or even think about bending down to field a ground ball. We can fix that.*' And I guess we can."

—⟨⟨⟩—

There's not much to say when a couple baseball guys down on their luck seek redemption in little more than a cosmic joke, prepared in triplicate by the law firm of Tweedy, Estes & Murchison of Providence, Rhode Island. But Pudge McAllister and Starchy Weldon, buffeted by the indifference of the baseball gods to the failings of mere mortals, found themselves forced to play the court jester.

They simply did what they had to do, and inked the one-year deal. Under the provisions of paragraph 3, lines 6 through 11:

> *Boyden Tinkerson McAllister [hereinafter BALLPLAY-ER] shall be excused from fielding, or attempting to field, all GROUND BALLS [hereinafter EXCLUSION] wheresoever hit on the field of play while in the employ of the Poquamscutt Harbor Chowda Bowls Professional Baseball Club, Inc. [hereinafter BALLCLUB]. Said EX-CLUSION shall NOT extend to bloopers, waist-high one-hoppers, or fly balls, whether foul or fair.*

Starchy handed Pudge his signed copy, and carefully tucked the other two into his desk drawer.

"Pudge, I got to be straight. You and I know that the Fates don't take kindly to screwing around with the game of baseball. Maybe I should just apologize to you, rip this contract up, and we both walk out of here and go for a beer and a couple plates of quahogs at a place I know, the Masked Mussel."

Starchy seemed to like that idea, at least for a long minute. Pudge had no idea what a quahog was, but kept that to himself. "Of course, maybe the owner's right and the fans will love it. But me? I just need to know one thing." Starchy looked out the window, where a tow-truck had just rolled in to pump some air in the rear tire of his tired Ford. *"Can you help me win the pennant?"*

—⁂—

The next afternoon, Pudge McAllister took the field for the Chowda Bowls.

Simple curiosity brought back the fans at first, the idea of some guy down on his luck bucking the whole system pleasing to the tough old mill hands and lobstermen and jocks of every kind with bad backs and impressive waists and sad stories of their own.

But Pudge soon became something more.

By August he was leading the Patriot League in home runs with 43, and batting .341. His hot bat more than made up for the inconvenient grounders that he simply passed up, or his waddling strolls to first base which turned sure extra-base hits into mere singles. He fielded without compromise or complaint the one-hoppers, bloopers, and flyballs required by his contract. This delighted the fans as well as the law firm of Tweedy, Estes & Murchison, which was keeping an eye on all things legal. The right fielder, the second baseman, and eventually most of the pitchers discovered that they could make a few easy adjustments to limit the other on-field damage caused by the no-ground-ball contract, and everyone soon joined in on the fun as the Chowda Bowls went on a torrid winning streak.

The team even hosted a few *"Fan and Clam Appreciation Days,"* with cups of thick chowder for a buck at the concession stand. The hot dog guy, who returned the second week of July like nothing had happened, tried adding a couple pint-sized containers of his mother's homemade clam chowder to his menu of flying hot dogs in the third inning of the first Appreciation event.

This was an error of judgment that could have been catastrophic had not Quincy Murchison, who had come over to the game from Providence with his law partners, jumped quickly to the cause and negotiated an immediate cash settlement with the not-so-easily amused, chowder-drenched fan sitting three rows behind him on the third base side.

By the end of the summer the stands were full, the organization in the black, and the owner looking to keep the team. On a cool evening three weeks after Labor Day, the Chowda Bowls needed a final win that would bring them the pennant, and they were playing the usually hapless Springfield Sprockets at home, the last game of the season.

—⚏—

Earlier in the game Pudge had singled in the second, walked in the fifth, and homered deep into right in the eighth for the Chowda Bowls only score. A chill mist had rolled in with the evening, and the damp outfield grass glistened under the old lights of the stadium. It was getting cold in Poquamscutt Harbor, although the announcer reported that a full-house of 17,354 paying customers had turned out for the last game of the season, along with eighteen retired Chowda Bowls players on a pass. Seven confused ladies of the Red Hat Society of Dedham, Massachusetts, also showed up, each clutching a promotional coupon which promised a seventh inning stretch appearance by Phil Collins.

While disappointed to learn that this was an unfortunate printing error, they were good sports about the whole thing, and one of the Red Hats even snagged a flying hot dog in the top of the eighth.

—⚏—

The scoreboard in left-center told the story, as scoreboards do.

The visiting Sprockets were up 2-1, the game well into the fifth hour. Pudge McAllister stood to the left of the plate, facing a 3-1 count in the bottom of the eleventh with one out and the tying run on second. The pitcher on the mound for the Sprockets was a second-year-kid out of Davidson named Spiffy Schill who had come in on relief in the ninth and thrown scoreless ball since.

Pudge tucked his shirt back in, his uniform noticeably loose on his now-slightly-less-than-Montana-sized frame, and stepped back into the box. Schill kicked up high on the mound, then fired a bullet which caught the outside corner of the plate. Pudge over-extended his swing, the pain shooting up his back.

"Steee-rike two!"

The favorite son of tiny Logan's Bluff, Georgia, who once had the big dreams, grimaced as he tapped the plate with his bat, took his stance, and said a prayer. It was short and to the point, like every prayer late in any game.

But as every ballplayer knows, there are always many prayers colliding around a ballpark, especially late in the game. It gets hard to hear them all, and the baseball gods seem to have a curious way of sorting them out when they do. Everybody who has ever played the game, or ever just watched a game, or even just launched free hot dogs and the occasional quart of clam chowder high into the stands of some old wooden stadium in a small town, knows this is rarely fair. It's just the way it is.

As Pudge McAllister fought the growing pain, Spiffy Schill nodded at his catcher, then kicked up high and fired a roundhouse curve that seemed to sweep in from somewhere left of Ohio.

Spiffy had said a prayer too.

Pudge began his swing, his bat glistening under the lights in the icy mist. But it was all wrong—off-balance and awkward and sad. As he completed his swing, he could hear—no, *feel*—the groan of the crowd as he missed the ball by half a foot, the pain now a scorching knife fight in his back.

Pudge McAllister had run the course, and he knew it. So did the fans.

They always do.

As he limped back to the dugout, the crowd rose to its feet. The ovation was long and heartfelt and bittersweet, muffled only by their damp gloves and the cold. He knew this was the walk all baseball players must take, sooner or later.

And maybe the rest of us, too.

Starchy was huddled in the corner of the dugout next to the bat rack, one foot up on the step. Pudge started to hand his bat to the batboy, but hesitated. He reached for a towel, painfully, and wiped the bat dry. He then put it away himself, in a space where the batboy had crossed out ~~Pudge~~, and written *TINK* in careful block letters just hours before the game.

The broken ballplayer turned to his manager. "Skipper, I'm done."

Starchy nodded. He seemed to know it too, and there was a sadness in his eyes. He turned back to the players now crowding the steps of the dugout. "It's all up to Smoltz now."

Gil Smoltz stepped up to the plate, a heavy-set catcher who had struggled with his own demons, the very same back-up catcher who had simply disappeared in the middle of the game in Pawtucket back in May. He had claimed temporary insanity, which at the time seemed entirely plausible. Against Starchy's protests he had been re-instated a week earlier, the boy-genius owner already working on a killer *Gil Smoltz Narrative* for the next year.

He took the first two pitches, wide and low. Schill shook off a couple signs, then fired a slider which didn't slide. The batter uncorked his compact frame, and his bat found the sweet-spot, just right.

The prayers of Gil Smoltz were floating around the chill air too.

The ball began its long, graceful climb into the mist of the night sky just as the lanky left-fielder for the Sprockets launched his own run to catch it, slipping for a second on the wet grass then sprinting to far left with his outstretched glove leading the way. Just as the ball started to fade foul a gust of wind nudged the ball back, and into the glove of the astonished left fielder...

—∞—

Joey's story had wound a bit long around the track, and my afternoon had slipped away with the last of the lunch crowd at the Masked Mussel. I thought my new friend had also wrung a little more out of the tale than it deserved, something my editor told me I did all the time, back when I had a real job.

Anyway, I sensed Joey was about to wrap it up.

"Yeah, I was right there that night, in the left-field bleachers." He shook his head. "That left-fielder was as surprised as anyone, I can tell you that. And that gust of wind that cost us the pennant? People around here will tell you *it came from nowhere. Yeah, that's what they say.*" He looked around, then shook his head. "But they're wrong, you know."

I didn't, at least not yet.

"Like I said, I was there, sitting high in left field that night as the gust blew in. It brushed by my left ear, and that's when I heard...*them.*" Joseph Caravaggio, an old lobsterman whose friends call him Joey and no longer goes to any night ball games, leaned in. "*The voices, that's what I heard. Voices in that gust of wind.*" He settled back into his chair. When he continued, his voice was barely above a whisper. "They sounded like a couple trying to keep a quarrel from the kids, that's how I remember it—cackling and laughing and damning any team which dared ride to a championship on something as wrong as a no-ground-ball-contract." Joey looked away, then back to me with a look more pleading than knowing. "I heard them that night. I did."

I liked the guy, and almost any baseball story over a couple beers. A little kindness never hurts either. "I'm sure you did, Joey."

He nodded. "Anyway, McAllister announced his retirement a few weeks later, after coming in second in the MVP voting with his .339 batting average and 52 homeruns, and he soon went back home to Georgia to coach at his old high school." Joey laughed, then shook his head. "He told some reporter up here he missed the tangy smell of the paper mills down South. No one had any idea what he was talking about."

I had grown up not far from a paper mill and understood, although it is not easy to explain and I didn't try.

"Not long after, the other owners got together and outlawed any provision of a contract which was '*inconsistent with the spirit of the game of baseball.*' That's how they put it." Joey shrugged. "It seems that the Commissioner had also heard that a couple jokers from some team over in Worcester had been talking to the law firm of Tweedy, Estes & Murchison about a contract provision allowing them to bring an emotional support animal to the dugout, one of them miniature horses, I think it was."

"That ban's probably a good idea, you know." I told him I had recently endured a flight sitting next to a middle-aged librarian and her support parrot. The three of us were squashed in an old single-aisle, two-by-two regional jet on a flight to Des Moines, the bird's vocabulary surprisingly robust, if annoyingly loud.

"Me, I never liked flying. That's why I drive over to those Cleveland games." Joey looked at his watch. "Well, I guess I took a little long to answer your question about why I don't like night games and bleacher seats."

A bit, I thought, but no matter. As I said, I love a baseball story.

"Just one more thing before you go. The League slapped an asterisk on McAllister's record with us, they did. After the little star it said, *'played one season with a no-ground-ball contract.'* "

"I guess they had to."

"Yeah, I guess they did." Joey took a last sip of his beer, thanked me for listening to an old lobsterman's story, and rose. As he walked away he hesitated, then turned around and smiled.

"You can't make this stuff up, you know."

Acknowledgments

Grateful acknowledgment is made to *Short Story America, Ebb & Flow, Reflections, Y'all Magazine,* and *Lowcountry Weekly,* where earlier versions of several of these stories first appeared.

The author also wishes to thank the Short Story America community of exceptional writers; the Wide Oak Writers, especially Jayne Adams and Rockelle Henderson; the St Augustine Writers Workshop, especially Connie May Fowler and Amanda Forbes Silva; the Island Writers Network; the Pat Conroy Literary Center, and especially Jonathan Haupt and Brooke McKinney; the South Carolina Writers Association; the Southeastern Writers Association; and the talented writers who have been more than generous with both their friendship and advance praise.

About the Author

Leaving the practice of law, with turns in the wheelhouse of several companies and teaching as an adjunct instructor at Michigan State, John W. "Mac" MacIlroy began writing creatively with a collaborative and well-received collection of "mostly, mostly true" stories of a zany boyhood *(www.notexactlyrocketscientists.com)*. Quickly realizing he had the attention span of a gerbil, he shelved a novel-in-progress and turned to short fiction, "stories told in tight places" as the critic Sam Sacks calls the short form. His early stories included "Duke's," which appeared in *Y'all Magazine* and was named a "Best of 2019 Short Story." Others followed, published in *Short Story America*, *Catfish Stew*, *Lowcountry Weekly*, *Short Fiction Break*, *Ebb & Flow*, and *Reflections*. His story "The Man Inside" was named a Finalist in both the 2021 Coker Fiction Fellowship and Excellence in Southern Lowcountry Writing competitions, and his story "Three Buses" was recognized as the winner of the 2021 Amy Munnell Prize. A graduate of Yale College, Harvard, and the University of Virginia School of Law, he lives along a Carolina tidal marsh with his wife Linda and a painted ceramic dodo bird named duMont.

9 781792 372308